LADY TANGLEWOOD: A NOVELLA

A SERVING MAGIC STORY

TONI CABELL

PREFACE

Lady Tanglewood is a standalone novella set in the world of Serving Magic that recounts the story of Nari Arlyss, the future Liege of Faynwood, as she prepares for her arranged marriage to the enigmatic son of a rival clan chief. What happens to Nari and her clan during a few brief days triggers the Faynwood Civil War, changing the trajectory of her life and those of future generations.

I pick up the threads of Nari's story fifty years later in *Lady Apprentice*, which follows the adventures of Nari's granddaughter and her friends. Linden Arlyss is headstrong, impulsive, and has a gift for getting into trouble, mostly the magical kind. Her story begins in Valerra, when the seeds of Fallow sorcery, planted in Faynwood so long ago, begin to take root in her homeland.

But for now, welcome to Faynwood, home of the five passionate, bickering Faymon clans, and their closest allies, the blue-haired, magical, interfering fays. Prepare to meet Nari and Mordahn on the cusp of their binding rites, when everything that could possibly go wrong does —with deadly consequences.

Content note: Lady Tanglewood has no spice, no swearing, and no gory violence. It's a suspenseful novella containing a high degree of emotional tension, a battle with swords and magic, and the loss of loved ones.

PREPARATION

PRYL

A DOG BARKED SOMEWHERE DOWN THE HALL, FOLLOWED BY A buoyant laugh that made Pryl's mouth go immediately dry. The dog's toenails scrambled on the wooden floorboards, clicking and slipping as he dashed after something, a ball probably, tossed by the owner of that glorious laughter.

Pryl inhaled deeply to steady his skittering pulse. *My reaction whenever she's near makes no rational sense. Why can't I rein in my rebellious heart? She. Is. Not. Mine. Her heart belongs to another, as unworthy as he may be.*

Pryl glanced up from his chair at the teakwood desk with a low growl of frustration. The slant of sunlight peeking through the tall windows indicated it was late afternoon. He'd been so absorbed he'd missed lunch entirely, his empty stomach grumbling an unhelpful reminder. But the Liege's library inside her longhouse was the finest in all of Faynwood, its booklined walls a welcome distraction to the dark visions that had been plaguing him of late.

A giant mastiff charged into the library, his tail wagging like a metronome, and dropped his ball next to Pryl, panting happily and dribbling on his polished boots. Pryl tossed down the quill he'd been using to document his latest findings, one more in a long list of depressing predictions regarding an imminent threat to Serving magic.

Normally he'd object to any interruptions when he was poring over the labyrinthine prophecies regarding the Liege of Faynwood, and more particularly, her only daughter, but his latest discovery was so alarming Pryl readily rolled up the scroll he'd been studying and set it aside on the desk. Then the subject of his scholarly research entered the library, and suddenly Pryl's shirt collar seemed two sizes too small.

The Liege's daughter was both stunning *and* smart, and she stole his breath away every time she walked into a room. Nari Arlyss was the most beautiful woman Pryl had ever encountered in any realm, human or fay. He lost the power of speech whenever she was around, which was why he always sought reasons to avoid her—as well as the fact she was promised to another.

Pryl cleared his throat, wishing he hadn't finished the tea one of the servants had brought him earlier. His throat was so parched he barely managed to croak out a greeting, "Good afternoon, Lady Tanglewood," using her official title as he bowed from the waist.

Nari, who wore a purple day gown, her blue-streaked, brunette hair falling softly to her shoulders, took a step back in surprise. Recovering herself, she bowed just as stiffly and formally as he had. "Good afternoon, Laird Archipryllius. Please forgive the intrusion. I'd thought you completed your studies for the day."

Pryl stared down at his boots in awkward silence, his mind having gone utterly blank. *Great stars above! What should I say? How can I engage Nari Arlyss in a normal conversation and demonstrate I'm not the fusty fay scholar she thinks I am?*

Nari waited a few beats, but when Pryl said nothing more, she gave him a polite smile and inclined her head. "Well, I can see you're ruminating over some great mystery, so I won't disturb you further."

Nari called out to her mastiff, "Come along, Quel. It's stopped raining so we can go outside."

She was almost out the door when Pryl blurted, "You can interrupt me anytime."

Nari turned toward him, a playful curve to her lips. "Even when you're reading one of those dusty old scrolls in the fay tongue?"

"Especially then."

Nari's dark eyes twinkled. "Very well. I shall be sure to bother you the next time your nose is buried in some ancient parchment." With a swish of her gown she was out the door.

Pryl's shoulders drooped in exhaustion; attempting to speak with Nari Arlyss was more wearying than spending a day transcribing old texts.

Someone slowly applauded behind him, and Pryl spun around with a scowl. "How long have you been hiding there?"

"I wasn't hiding...and I've been here long enough to see you behaving like a smitten school boy instead of a respected fay prince." Nari's fay tutor, Mage Pawllah, shook her head at him, her top-knot of bright blue braids bouncing as if to emphasize her point.

Pryl crossed his arms. "Fays haven't had a monarchy it more than a millennia, so technically I can't be a fay prince."

"Technically, you *are* a fay prince, although we no longer recognize the title in our realm."

"Fine," Pryl waved his hand. "What's your point?"

"That you need to behave like the future fay chief and stop pining. Nari Arlyss is due to be married in less than two months!"

"To an absolute horse's fanny," sputtered Pryl, his mood darkening every time he thought of Nari's fiancé.

"That's not for you to say. Besides, you're just jealous she's not completing the rites of binding with you instead."

Pryl ignored the comment about his jealousy, which was true. He knew he'd be a far better husband to Nari because he loved her with his whole being. Could her betrothed, with his slipshod magic skills and fondness for hunting wild boars, make the same claim? Oh, the man was dashing to be sure, but he was also arrogant and potentially unstable. "You can't possibly tell me you approve of Commander Mordahn?"

"I'm neutral, for now. And while I have little regard for his father, Chief Orbahn, I will give his son the benefit of the doubt. The match is politically astute, and Nari seems quite fond of him."

Pryl huffed out a sigh. "But is Mordahn Erewin loyal to Serving magic? Will he remain true to the way or veer off into Fallow sorcery?" *And will he love, honor, and protect Nari all her days?*

Pawllah furrowed her brow. "We must allow the future to write itself, and we must be prepared to protect Nari Arlyss should Mordahn Erewin prove himself unworthy."

"On that last point we're in complete accord," said Pryl. "I will be watching Mordahn like an eagle over her fledgling—one false move, and I will not hesitate to intervene."

APPREHENSION

NARI

Nari shifted in the saddle, stiff and sore from a week on the road. She looked forward to spending time with her fiancé and visiting his Arrowood clan. Their formal rites of binding would be completed during the Midsummer festival in six weeks. Nari's stomach fluttered nervously every time she thought about her pending wedding. This trip to Arrowood would be the last official visit between the two clans until the ceremony itself, which would occur in her parents' Tanglewood stronghold. The two families still had wedding plans to discuss, including the final dowry details.

Nari traveled the road to Arrowood with nine others from her clan: her parents, three fays, and four servants. The fays in their party technically weren't from Tanglewood, although Nari's fay tutor, Pawllah, had been a part of her life for as long as she could remember. Nari's father, Selden, led the Tanglewood clan, and her mother, Ayala, was the Faymon Liege. Ayala oversaw magical and military matters for all the clans.

With the long trip, nerves were beginning to fray all around. Nari heard her parents arguing about something as they rode side by side. Since her parents rarely disagreed about anything, Nari decided to intercede. She waited until the road widened and then pulled her palomino alongside her mother's mare. "What's wrong? You've been arguing since our last rest stop."

"Nothing's wrong." Ayala shook her head, her long braid swishing with the movement. Her chestnut brown hair glinted with the characteristic blue highlights that every Faymon, regardless of their clan or status, shared in common. Faymons were ninety-eight percent human and two percent fay, their blue-streaked hair a reminder of their fay ancestry. Fays had one hair color: vivid blue. Their men's beards grew blue as well. Even among fay elders, not a hint of silver ever threaded through their bright blue locks.

Nari drew her brows together. "I have ears, and you and Father have been 'debating' for the past two hours. Is it about the rites of binding?"

Selden glanced at his daughter, his blue eyes clouded. "This is nothing for you to worry about." Whenever her father said that Nari knew she had *something* to worry about. She also knew she'd learn nothing from her parents by taking a direct approach.

Nari sighed. "I thought the two of you approved of my marriage to Mordahn." Last year, a few months before Nari turned sixteen, Arrowood's ambassador had brokered the marital arrangement between Mordahn, son of the Arrowood clan chief, and Nari, promising it would tie their clans more closely together. While Ayala and Selden had agreed in principle, they insisted this had to be a love union between the two young people.

Nari appreciated Mordahn's intellect and his commitment to Serving magic, which all Faymons were sworn to uphold. Right from their very first meeting, she found they were well suited in terms of background and interests, from gardening and horseback riding, to preferring mastiffs above any other dog breed. Mordahn always seemed slightly in awe of Nari's magical gifts, which she had to confess were more disciplined than his. Of course, Nari had the advantages of a fay tutor and two powerful master mages for parents. Plus, Nari practiced her Serving magic spells all the time, whereas Mordahn preferred hunting and fishing to studying his spell book.

Over the past year, Nari's attraction to Mordahn had grown. Her pulse quickened whenever his dark eyes locked onto hers, the intensity in his gaze sometimes causing her to blush. Her stomach lightened every time his lips brushed her hand, and once, when he'd caught her in a private moment without a chaperone, he'd sealed his lips over hers. Heat had flooded through her veins at his kiss. Nari was certain she'd fallen in love.

Earlier that spring, when her mother had asked whether she wanted to proceed with the rites of binding, Nari had given her consent. However, she knew as well as anyone their two clans had uneasy relations. Her

Tanglewood clan had been the ruling clan for generations; her own mother, as the Faymon Liege, had ultimate authority over the clan chiefs, including Mordahn's father. The Arrowood chief had always chafed somewhat under her mother's authority. Nari didn't know whether it was due to her mother's gender, or the fact that Arrowood wasn't in charge of everything.

Ayala smiled, her eyes crinkling at the corners. "Of course we approve. We wouldn't be traveling all this way if we hadn't reached an accord before now. As your father said, nothing should concern you, except your wedding plans. I confess I won't rest easy until I see your gown for the ceremony. The first fitting left something to be desired, don't you think?"

While Nari knew her mother was trying to distract her, she had to admit that talking about her wedding and her new clothes, especially her gown, was a worthy distraction. Nari chuckled. "I fear we may need to use magic if the next fitting goes as poorly."

"I have a feeling the next fitting will be a vast improvement." Ayala grinned. "I'm more concerned about the rites of binding. Every clan chief is sending a large party—we'll need to set up tree houses in the woods to accommodate everyone!" Nari and her parents laughed, easing some of the earlier tension she'd detected between them. She saw that the trail narrowed ahead, and she dropped behind them once again. As she rode, she made mental lists in her head of everything she had to discuss with Mordahn, from the color of the entryway tiles for their new longhouse, to the fruit trees they wanted to plant in their garden.

Nari noticed a cloud of dust in the distance and shouted to her parents, "Riders are heading this way, a sizable group if the swirls of dust are any indication."

Selden brought a hand up to his brow to block out the glare of the sun. "Looks like Arrowood colors."

"Do you see Mordahn?" asked Nari, leaning forward in her saddle.

Selden shrugged. "I should think not," he called over his shoulder. "We still have a full day's ride ahead of us before reaching his father's stronghold."

The sound of horses' hooves drowned out any further conversation, as a contingent of clansmen, bearing the green and brown colors of the Arrowood clan, galloped toward them. Linden recognized her future father-in-law, Chief Orbahn, at the head of the group.

"Welcome, Tanglewood clan! Welcome to the forests of Arrowood!" boomed Orbahn, riding toward Nari and her parents on his bay stallion. Nari wondered why Orbahn would bother greeting them out here, pretty much in the middle of nowhere, rather than wait for her clan to arrive at his stronghold tomorrow. Not that she minded, so long as Mordahn had come along with his father. Otherwise, this would be a dull ride through Arrowood territory.

Orbahn reined in his horse, whose nose was nearly touching Ayala's mare. "Well met, Liege Ayala and Chief Selden," he rasped. "We expected you earlier." Nari sensed a subtle shift in her father's posture, his muscles tensing across his back. Although she sat behind him, she knew Selden's strong chin would be clenched in silent anger at Orbahn's affront. No one, not even the chief of a neighboring clan, dared to approach the Faymon Liege so closely without permission. Wars had been fought over such offenses in the past.

"Well met, Chief Orbahn." Ayala nodded. "'Tis true, we ran into a spot of bad weather that delayed us somewhat."

Nari arched an eyebrow at Ayala's tone—decidedly chilly, wary even. *What's behind Mother's attitude toward Orbahn? Is it because he approached her way too closely? And why is Orbahn riding out to greet us so far from his home? None of this makes sense.*

Nari had never really liked her future father-in-law. The looks Orbahn gave her sometimes, when he didn't think she was watching, made her feel soiled somehow, unworthy. She stopped thinking about Orbahn when a ruggedly handsome young man greeted her parents with a polite bow, and then skirted around them to join Nari.

"Lady Tanglewood, welcome to humble Arrowood. It does my heart good to see you again," said Mordahn, a smile playing on his lips as he pulled his black horse alongside Nari's palomino. He used Nari's formal title, as befitting the Faymon Liege's daughter. Tall, broad chested, exuding confidence, Mordahn sat erect in his saddle, his eyes twinkling as he smiled down at her. Sometimes Nari thought Mordahn was a tad over-confi-dent, almost bordering on arrogant. She'd confessed as much to her tutor, who told Nari to give him time. Young men of twenty were often arrogant, especially when betrothed to the Liege's daughter.

Mordahn's sandy-colored hair, lightly dusted with blue, grazed the collar of his tunic. His dark eyes, guarded with everyone else, softened when he gazed at Nari. She nodded at Orbahn and the other Arrowood clansmen who'd ridden out to greet them. All wore battledress, Mordahn included, their silver chainmail gleaming whenever the sun peeked through the tall trees overhead. By contrast, none of the Tanglewood clan wore armor, opting for more comfortable traveling clothes. Nari's aubergine cape flapped in the spring breeze. Beneath her cape she wore a lavender riding dress with gold piping, the long skirt split so as not to constrict her in the saddle.

"What a lovely surprise, Commander," Nari smiled. As Orbahn's son and second-in-command, Mordahn would one day be Chief of Arrowood. Nari believed he would be a more compassionate leader than his father, who ruled Arrowood with an iron fist. Despite Orbahn's reputation for dealing harshly with any who crossed him, he'd always been loyal to Ayala and Selden. "I appreciate the warm welcome, but why have you come all this way, and with so many clansmen dressed for battle?"

Mordahn waved his gloved hand at the woods surrounding them. "We've had a number of wolf sightings in these parts. Father wanted to ensure you and your parents arrived safely at the stronghold."

"Oh," said Nari, who didn't think they needed twenty-four clansmen to defend them from a wolf attack. After all, they had three fays traveling with them, and fays could easily cast protection wards around them, or even transport them out of harm's way. And her mother and father, as master mages, were more than able to cast a defensive shield around them. Even if their magic failed, which had never happened, everyone from Tanglewood could wield a sword as well as they could cast a spell.

But Nari didn't want to seem ungrateful, given the effort her fiancé and his father had made, so she smiled. "Thank you for going to so much trouble on our behalf."

Mordahn's voice grew husky. "No amount of effort is too much when it comes to keeping my betrothed safe. You should know by now how I feel about you."

Nari's pulse raced, which happened every time Mordahn spoke of his feelings. Sometimes he sounded almost possessive, but she brushed aside the thought. Changing the subject, she asked, "How fares your little brother? Has he learned his basic spells yet?"

Mordahn shared a few amusing stories about his brother's magical misfires, both of them laughing over the young boy's antics. Nari's father joined them, and the conversation shifted to the best spots for hunting and fishing in their respective provinces. When Selden and Mordahn began swapping tales on the largest trout ever caught, or the biggest elk ever spotted, Nari dropped back to ride with her tutor.

Pawllah turned her head and smiled, her pearly teeth

a pretty contrast to her deep brown complexion. The small fay woman divided her waist-length hair into half a dozen blue braids, which she twisted on top of her head, creating a tall, intricate top bun. Nari was convinced Pawllah held her hair in place with magic. Like the other fays in their group, she wore a long cape over her riding tunic and slacks, her clothes made from a silvery, stretchy fay fabric.

Officially, the fay woman was Nari's tutor, responsible for educating Nari in Serving magic, as well as the other subjects the Liege's daughter would need to master, everything from literature and history to negotiation and diplomacy. But Pawllah was also Nari's companion and closest friend. When Mordahn once suggested to Nari she would no longer need her tutor after their marriage, Nari had stormed out of the receiving room of her parents' longhouse. Mordahn quickly relented, although Nari noticed he rarely met Pawllah's eyes. Once or twice, she'd caught Mordahn scowling at something Pawllah said.

When Nari mentioned it to Pawllah, the fay had chuckled in her tinkling way. "Aye, I don't believe the young Arrowood commander could have foreseen that his lovely bride came along with fay baggage—a nosy, opinionated fay at that!"

Nari chewed her bottom lip as she rode alongside her tutor. Pawllah glanced at her a few times, finally shaking her head. "What's on your mind, lass? If you keep masticating your mouth like that, your fiancé will have nothing left to kiss."

Nari rolled her eyes. "I'm wondering why Orbahn rode out here to greet us, a day's ride from his stronghold, bringing a posse of Arrowood warriors with him, all dressed for battle."

"Did you ask your fiancé that question?"

"Aye," said Nari, compressing her lips into a thin line.

"Well don't leave me in suspense. What did he say?"

When Nari related Mordahn's explanation of wolves in the area, it was Pawllah's turn to roll her eyes. "The commander may be the only one among us who believes that explanation. Ride on ahead and I'll catch up. I want to check in with the others."

By "others," Nari knew she meant the other fays in their group. Pawllah slowed her horse to a gentle trot, allowing the other two fays to catch up with her. The three of them conferred in their ancient buzzing language, which sounded like a hive of bees to untrained ears. They spoke rapidly, the sound of horses' hooves striking the ground drowning out much of their exchange. Nari's ears picked up a stray word here and there, "Trust...stay...magic."

Nari didn't hear anything that alarmed her. Besides, she knew she tended to be too critical, too quick to pass judgment. Shrugging, she decided to relax and enjoy the extra time with Mordahn, who rejoined her on the road. They passed the time pleasantly, talking about their upcoming rites of binding and the accompanying week-long celebration, and the new longhouse Mordahn was building for the two of them and their household staff. Nari still found it hard to believe she'd be running a household soon, harder still to accept she'd be living so far from her parents and friends in Tanglewood. She swallowed down the lump forming in her throat, nostalgia for her happy childhood, nearly spent, threatening to overwhelm her.

Since the afternoon sun was waning, and no one traveled the Arrowood road after nightfall, Orbahn sent half his clansmen ahead to set up a campsite. The four Tanglewood servants accompanied them. When the rest of the party arrived at the campsite, their tents had been erected and several campfires started, cauldrons bubbling over the fires. Nari hadn't realized she was hungry until the savory scents of stewing meat and root vegetables wafted toward her.

She waved goodbye to Mordahn, following her parents to the tents. Tanglewood's smaller enclave had been set up in the center of the campsite, with a ring of Arrowood tents surrounding theirs. This was unusual, and Nari wondered why her mother and father didn't immediately object. Typically, traveling clan chiefs signaled their independence and at times, wariness, by establishing separate campsites. Different clans may share meals together on the road, but never intermingled campsites. Even when all five Faymon clans gathered for the magic trials every two years, they set up five independent enclaves.

"Nari, come join your father and me. We'd like a word before dinner." Ayala pointed to the tent she shared with Selden. Although the Liege generally traveled with a ceremonial tent, large enough to host council meetings inside, Ayala had elected to leave her cavernous tent at home. Otherwise, they would have needed twice as many pack animals and servants to transport the tent and its contents, which included an ornately carved bed, a low table that could seat twenty, wall hangings, area rugs, and an abundance of linens and pillows.

The three fays followed behind Nari, the six of them squeezed inside her parents' tent, which had been designed for two people, three at the most. "What's going on?" hissed Selden as soon as they'd cleared the doorway. "This affront is worse than the first one." Nari knew her father was referring to the positioning of their much smaller enclave inside the Arrowood camp, effectively swallowing up the Tanglewood clan. Orbahn had now offended Liege Ayala and Chief Selden twice in one afternoon. *That must be some kind of record*, thought Nari.

The quietest of the three fays, a young man in his early twenties, stepped forward. Pryl was lean and muscular, with shale gray eyes and wavy blue hair that curled over the collar of his tunic. He was striking, with his chiseled chin and sculpted cheekbones, a handsome, almost ethereal quality to his face. The only son of Chief Archipryllius Orion the Thirteenth, Pryl had joined their household several months earlier. He was serving as the unofficial fay ambassador for the next year. Although the Faymon Liege historically had cordial relations with the fays, Ayala had gone a step further. She sought a closer alliance with the fay chief by inviting his son and heir into her inner circle.

Nari had tried to befriend Pryl when he first arrived

in Tanglewood, but she'd found him to be shy, almost standoffish, rarely meeting her eyes. Unfailingly polite, he bowed whenever he addressed her, always using her formal title, Lady Tanglewood. Every time he bowed, she of course returned the bow, bending at the waist at precisely the same angle, so as not to give offense. After all, they were of equal standing; Pryl would one day lead the fays, and she would one day lead the Faymons.

After several attempts at engaging Pryl in conversation, Nari stopped trying. The future chief of the fays was either too serious or saddened by some event in his past, or perhaps foreseen in his future, to engage in small talk. Pawllah told her Pryl's mother had died when he was quite young, followed by his stepmother more recently. It could have been those losses, but Nari thought it had something to do with the prophetic scrolls he spent much of his free time studying. She'd be depressed too if that's all she did every day.

Nari's mother had been born a revelator, both a mage and seer in equal balance, a rare combination. While all mages had occasional visions, and all seers could perform basic spells, a revelator must learn to master both powerful gifts. The only other revelator Nari knew of was her fiancé, although Mordahn would be the first to admit he'd not mastered either of his gifts. He was a mage of average abilities, not yet a master, and his visions were so confounding that he told Nari he'd quite given up trying to decipher them.

Ayala had been plagued with bad dreams and visions of late. She had once explained to Nari that her visions could be images from the past or the present, or they could be the shades of things that might come to pass but might not. Nari found the whole field of prophecy too fanciful for her. Old scrolls held little interest for her, much to Pawllah's chagrin. Her fay tutor, like Pryl, studied the scrolls and prophecies, believing they contained versions of the truth. Pawllah would tut-tut whenever Nari made fun of the old seers, who liked nothing better than predicting doom and gloom for the next fifty years.

Pryl cleared his throat, his gray eyes clouded with worry. "It's as you suspect, my Liege. These woods reek of Fallow sorcery, of dark magic and forbidden deeds."

Ayala rounded on the young fay. "Are absolutely you certain?" When Pryl nodded, she turned to Pawllah and the third fay in their group, Elanya. The fay women spoke as one, "Aye, 'tis a Fallow place."

Ayala rubbed her hands up and down the sleeves of her riding dress, her brow furrowed. "What is Orbahn up to? How does he employ this sorcery?"

Pryl stared down at his tall boots, rubbing the blue stubble on his chin. "It's something to do with wolves and...and death." He glanced up, his eyes settling on Nari, a stricken expression on his handsome face. Pryl shook his head and looked away, waving his hand at Pawllah.

The fay tutor picked up the thread. "While we're certain Orbahn is lying about the reason for meeting us in the most isolated section of Arrowood, something about the wolves does worry him."

"But how could wolves pose a serious threat?" asked Selden impatiently. "A whole pack is still no match for our magic."

"It's not the wolves themselves, or their number, but rather what they could reveal that scares Orbahn," said Elanya, the oldest of the fays and Pawllah's cousin. A woman on the far side of fifty, she wore her blue hair pulled back in a severe bun.

"Scared? Why would Orbahn be frightened, if he is the one invoking Fallow magic?" asked Selden, his jaw clenched in frustration. Nari knew her father well, and everything about his rigid posture and the way he curled and uncurled his fists told her he was more than frustrated. He was frightened as well, but why?

Nari knew the fays could whisk them out of harm's way in a moment on their traveling mists. Perhaps Selden was simply unsure how to proceed, which didn't happen often to the Chief of Tanglewood. His wife and daughter—the current Liege and future Liege of the five Faymon clans of Faynwood—were far from home, surrounded by Orbahn's clan, and potentially in danger. Nari wanted to reassure her father, tell him all would be well, but something held her back, her own fears and doubts perhaps.

Pryl exhaled, and careful to avoid Nari's eyes, turned to Selden. "Orbahn wants to ensure nothing interferes with the rites of binding between his son and Lady Tanglewood. Something about these woods, and these wolves, causes him great worry."

Selden reached out to Nari, gripping her hands in his

much larger ones. "My dear girl, think now. Has Mordahn ever given you cause for concern? I speak now of his loyalties to Serving magic."

Nari shook her head, her voice certain. "No, Father. Mordahn has always expressed his devotion to Serving magic. Whenever he casts spells, they are clear and true, without a hint of dark magic."

Ayala said, "So Orbahn's Fallow ways have not polluted his son. That's something to be grateful for, at least."

Pryl coughed, and Ayala spun around, her eyes boring into Pryl's. "What is it, Pryl? You must speak freely, while there's still time." Her mother crossed her arms, as if trying to ward off whatever the young fay was about to say.

"Time for what?" asked Nari, confused by her mother's words. A gloomy shroud seemed to settle around Nari's heart. *Is this a warning perhaps, of darkness ahead, or simply fanciful thinking?* Nari shook herself, unwilling to dwell in stories and prophecies that may never come true.

"Time to call off the rites of binding," said Selden quietly, his voice quivering with emotion. "It would be wise to remember that Arrowood has dabbled in Fallow magic before, wreaking havoc among the clans and costing countless lives."

Nari shook her head. "But that was over a hundred years ago, and the entire clan suffered for it. Surely they've learned their lesson by now!"

"If Chief Orbahn has fallen into Fallow ways, then

you cannot—you must not—marry his son," said Selden firmly. "I will not allow my daughter to be contaminated. Nor can we risk inviting even a whiff of dark sorcery into our clan. If Tanglewood falls away from Serving magic, so falls all of Faynwood."

Tanglewood's position as the ruling clan required strict adherence to the ways of Serving magic. As the future Liege, Nari would be expected to protect Faynwood and Serving magic at all costs. If she ever needed to choose between her fiancé and Serving magic, Nari knew she really had no choice. Serving magic was the one true path, which she was sworn to uphold.

Nari sputtered, "But Mordahn is innocent, I'm sure of it. How can you even suggest breaking our vows?" She turned on her heels, ready to storm out of the tent, but Pryl reached out and touched her arm, his hand closing around her wrist. "Stay, Lady Tanglewood, please. Search your own heart and tell me you are not suspicious of Chief Orbahn, uncomfortable even."

Nari's arm seemed to catch fire at Pryl's touch. He'd never approached her so closely before, always maintaining at least an arm's length distance. Her face flushed at his nearness, her heart trembling in her chest. She noticed, really noticed, the young fay for the first time: the planes of his face, the cool gray eyes, the tightly wound muscles, and the otherworldly presence. Startled by her reaction, Nari shook off Pryl's hand, wishing for all the world she could retreat to her own tent and turn over what just happened to her, the strange flutterings triggered by Pryl's touch.

Nari expelled a puff of air. She didn't want to concede her misgivings about Orbahn, but she couldn't lie to her parents. "'Tis true, I don't like Orbahn. But his son is nothing like him."

"Not yet anyway." Bowing his head, Pryl folded his long, graceful fingers in front of him.

Selden narrowed his eyes. "You've been studying the prophecies for months. Do they coincide with your visions?" When Pryl nodded, Selden urged, "Tell us what you've seen, please."

Pryl's head remained bowed, and he stared down at the floor of the tent. His voice grew distant, as if he were reciting a dream from some far-off realm. "I've seen war among the clans, decades of fighting and loss. Fallowness will take root in Arrowood and spread, destroying many lives in its wake. We risk losing all of Faynwood, and Serving magic along with it." Pryl snapped his head up and stared into Nari's eyes. "Mordahn's future is clouded, his path uncertain. I have seen him as a loyal Serving mage, and as a ruthless Fallow sorcerer. What happens here and now, in this forest, will seal his fate—and ours."

Nari brought her hands up to cover her ears. "Just stop. I refuse to hear any more of this nonsense." Where she'd been attracted to Pryl moments earlier, now she was furious at him for spouting his prophetic visions about Mordahn and Fallow sorcery, and at her parents for taking it all so seriously.

Nari felt her mother reach up from behind and gently

pry Nari's hands from her ears. "You must listen to Pryl," whispered Ayala, "and to me."

Nari spun around toward her mother. Worry lines creased Ayala's pale brow, and the dark smudges beneath her eyes told of sleepless nights. Nari recalled her parents arguing earlier, on the road to Arrowood. Suddenly, the source of their disagreement became clear to her. Knowing her mother, Ayala would have wanted to tell Nari about her worries concerning Fallow magic inside Arrowood, probably even before they left home. Selden would have nixed the idea, trying to protect his "little girl" a while longer. This trip to Arrowood, to complete the final wedding planning details, had a much more serious underlying purpose: to discover whether Fallowness had taken root again in Arrowood, and if so, to uncover the dark mage before it was too late.

Nari's voice hitched as she asked her mother, "Your dreams?"

Ayala nodded. "Too similar to Pryl's visions to be a coincidence."

Nari's shoulders slumped, exhaustion overtaking her. *If Orbahn has become what they believe, if he has turned from Serving magic to Fallow sorcery, could I marry Mordahn? Would I even want to, if the slightest chance exists the son might follow in his father's footsteps?* Nari shuddered at the thought. Running her hand through her blue-streaked hair, the same chestnut shade as her mother's, she sighed. "What evidence do we have of Orbahn's misdeeds? I admit his behavior is off putting, but that's not proof he's become a Fallow mage."

Selden gave Nari a wistful smile. "My daughter asks a wise question, befitting a future leader. If we are to break off the rites of binding now, so close to the actual ceremony, we need evidence. Otherwise we risk offending the entire Arrowood clan."

Ayala nodded. "Aye. For now, I suggest we act normally. Let's keep our eyes and ears open, and our magic focused on discovering the source of Fallowness we sense in these woods. Perhaps it's not Orbahn at all, but a mage in his employ. A single bad apple in the barrel we could pluck out without damaging the rest."

Nari thought her mother added the last part to help her feel better. But between the looks Orbahn gave her, and his behavior that afternoon, Nari worried he may have already turned down the dark path.

DECEPTION

NARI

"Nari," called Mordahn. He stood outside Nari's small tent. "Come, everyone else is seated."

Nari had been ready for a quarter hour, but she couldn't bring herself to leave the tent. She'd scrubbed her face and hands twice to rid them of the dust from the road. After sending her maidservant to assist with the dinner, Nari brushed out all the pins the woman had painstakingly put in her hair, electing to leave her waves loose about her shoulders. She checked her reflection one last time, and remembering to smile, she said, "I'll be right out."

Mordahn would know immediately something was wrong if she weren't careful to hide the emotions roiling inside her. As the daughter of Liege Ayala, who was well known for her skill as a master negotiator, Nari had been taught from an early age to master her emotions, especially when facing uncertain situations. Nari pulled aside her tent flap, her face impassive, and looked up at Mordahn. "I'm sorry I kept you waiting."

Mordahn smiled. "I don't mind waiting for you. You must be tired from a week on the road. At least you'll be able to sleep in a proper bed tomorrow night." He looped her arm through his and led her over to the campfires. He'd managed to save a spot for the two of them that was somewhat removed from the rest. Once she was seated, he waved his hand at two Arrowood clansmen, who served them steaming bowls of meat stew over potato mash, and mugs of mulled wine.

Nari forced down a small amount of food, her stomach so knotted she couldn't manage any more. Mordahn looked at her uneaten dinner and frowned. He knew she was a hearty eater; Nari had never been one to pick delicately at her food when her fiancé was around, and then rush to the kitchen later to satisfy her hunger. "What's wrong?" he asked quietly. "Is it your father?"

Nari picked up her mulled wine and took a sip, stalling for time. She took another swallow, the wine tasting slightly metallic on her tongue. Arrowood's vintners could learn much from Tanglewood. "My father? Whatever do you mean?"

"Selden's eyes have been filled with storm clouds since we met on the road, and once or twice, I saw him gritting his teeth at my father. Why?"

Nari decided she'd have to navigate this carefully, tell the truth mostly, without revealing her parents' suspicions about Orbahn. She reminded Mordahn that

Faymon customs forbade anyone from approaching the Liege as closely as Orbahn had, without first asking permission. Mordahn chuckled. "Is that all? Why, we are practically family."

Nari continued. "Then there's the matter of our campsite being set up inside Arrowood's enclave, which is highly irregular, as you well know."

Mordahn nodded. "True, but my father wanted to ensure you and your parents would be safe from the wolves as you slept."

"What kind of wolves are these? Wouldn't a protection ward do the trick?"

Mordahn shrugged. "Several of our clansmen have spotted an unusually large, aggressive wolf pack roaming these woods at night. A caravan of traveling merchants was attacked not far from here last week, and one family was dragged from their tent and killed."

"That's horrible." Nari wanted to believe this story of aggressive wolves in the area, but she questioned the veracity of such a tall tale. Even if it were true, Serving magic would more than suffice in any "battle" with wolves. "Are any of these clansmen here tonight? I'd like to question them myself about this wolf pack."

Mordahn shifted uneasily on the ground and refused to look at her directly. *Ah, he's covering up for his father. He knows more than he's revealing. So I will play by the same rules.*

"None of the eyewitnesses are here tonight." Mordahn held up his empty mug. "Be right back. Do you need anything, my love?"

Shaking her head, Nari watched him leave. He stopped once or twice for a quick chat with a clansman before refilling his mulled wine. Mordahn was definitely holding back on her, but she was holding back on him too. They were both protecting their clans, but Nari was protecting more than Tanglewood. If what Pryl and Ayala believed about Orbahn's fall into Fallow sorcery turned out to be true, she was protecting Serving magic itself.

After dinner, an Arrowood clansman brought out his fiddle, another her flute, and they played several bawdy tunes, a few of the clansmen dancing and laughing to their lively music. When they finished, Ayala invited Pryl to contribute. He went to his tent and returned with a small, stringed instrument, the fay equivalent of a lyre. As he strummed the strings, the entire campsite grew quiet, everyone settling down, the lyre's notes both sweet and melancholy. Pryl sang an old ballad, a favorite of Pawllah's, about a pair of star-crossed lovers.

Nari leaned forward, drawn by the haunting melody and lyrics, and by Pryl's baritone, his voice rich and soothing. He must have sensed her watching and glanced up. Their eyes locked, his face softening as he gazed at her. Nari felt herself wrapped in a velvety cocoon, warm and safe. It was an offering, of loyalty and friendship, and more if she wished, hers for the asking. She tilted her head to one side and Pryl nodded. The spell, if that's what it was, broke, and she felt a pang of loss, so deep and cutting she gasped. A similar wave of melancholy washed over his handsome features, and

Pryl's voice wavered. He dropped his eyes, his fingers gliding effortlessly over the lyre as he reached the ballad's last stanza.

Nari found herself distracted, only half-listening to Mordahn, who tensed beside her. He glanced across the camp at Pryl, crinkling his brow. "How well do you know that yodeling fay prince?" Mordahn's voice, laced with sarcasm, grated on Nari's already frayed nerves.

Could Mordahn possibly be jealous? Nari didn't want to rouse her fiancé's suspicions when he had no cause for concern, at least not because of Pryl. His father's dalliances in Fallow sorcery, if true, were another story. She shrugged, striking a casual tone. "Not very well. He spends most of the time in the library back home, reading and studying."

Mordahn squared his jaw. "I don't want him around us after we're wed. I can tolerate Pawllah well enough, for your sake, but I'm no fan of the fays. Too sneaky by half."

Nari stiffened, his words deeply insulting. "You are very much mistaken about the fays."

Mordahn backpedaled. "I don't mean to offend. I know Tanglewood puts great stock in their relations with the fays. Arrowood has not found the fays quite so... generous with their time and talents."

Mordahn pivoted to other, lighter topics, even telling a few funny stories at his own expense. The tension between them eased, as the man she'd come to know and care about resurfaced. Chuckling and feeling surer of herself, and of Mordahn, than she had all day, Nari started to relax. Her eyes grew heavy with the wine and the warmth of the fire. Stifling a yawn, she rose from the ground. Mordahn stood with her and leaned over to kiss her cheek. She bid him goodnight and paused long enough on the way to her tent to wish Orbahn and her parents a good evening. Ayala gave Nari a smile that didn't reach her eyes.

Nari noticed the Tanglewood tents had been rearranged while everyone was at dinner, although they were still embedded within the Arrowood enclave. Her parents' tent and hers sat side-by-side, and directly opposite were three tents, one for each fay. All five tents faced inward, with a small amount of ground between for privacy. The tents of the four servants were set up around the perimeter, one at each corner, and their flaps faced outward.

Nari heard footsteps and glanced between the tents, unsure what to make of the new arrangement. She heard a familiar cough and exhaled in relief. "Pryl, is that you?"

Pryl emerged from the shadows beyond their row of tents, carrying a small fireball in his palm to light the way. "Aye, Lady Tanglewood. I've just finished with the tents."

He addressed her with his usual formality and peered down at his boots as he spoke. Nari didn't know what to make of Pryl, or whatever had passed between them, but she was exhausted and needed to get some sleep. She waved her hand. "Why did you rearrange the tents? And why so close together?"

Pryl cleared his throat. "'Tis more secure this way,

my lady. Sleep well. I will keep watch." He held his fire-ball aloft and waited for her to enter her tent. She pulled aside the flap and turned around, nodding goodnight. Pryl gathered his silver cape around himself and sat cross-legged just inside his tent entrance, diagonally opposite hers. He placed his sword on the ground next to him and let his fireball wink out.

Nari ignored the white nightgown her maidservant had thoughtfully laid out on her bedroll. She'd not be wearing that tonight, not if Pryl felt the need to guard her sleep. Sorting through her saddlebag, she pulled out a pair of navy leggings and a long, stretchy, pale blue tunic with tiny navy stars and crescent moons stitched into the fabric.

Nari wore tunics and leggings for fencing practice, for running through the gardens with Quel, her mastiff, and for climbing her favorite tree back home. She preferred tunics and leggings to dresses and skirts and owned many varieties and colors, all stored in the trunk at the foot of her Tanglewood bed, except for the blue set she'd smuggled into her bag at the last moment. Ayala wouldn't approve; it was one thing for Nari to wear leggings or trousers when in the privacy of her family's longhouse, quite another while in Arrowood, visiting her fiancé's clan.

Nari quickly changed, repacked her saddlebag, and pulled her aubergine cape around her shoulders. She reclined on top of her bedroll, with her boots on her feet. Placing her sword on the floor beside her, she turned onto her side. Nari listened to the low buzz of conversation, occasionally punctuated with laughter, from the men and women still gathered around the campfires. She found it hard to believe any of them practiced Fallow magic. They all seemed so friendly and normal.

Her mind drifted to the sharp contrast between the fay chief's son and the clan chief's son: Pryl was slim, muscular, classically handsome, with a natural grace to every movement; Mordahn was tall, broad-shouldered, ruggedly good-looking, with an authoritative air that demanded attention. Of the two men, Mordahn was definitely the more commanding, the one every man or woman noticed in a crowd.

However, her unexpected reaction to Pryl forced her to reevaluate the man he was, and the friend he promised to be. Having the future fay chief as a loyal ally was no small thing. Whatever their future alliance might entail, she would complete the rites of binding with Mordahn as planned, assuming his father hadn't turned to Fallow sorcery and darker paths. Nari thought her mother and the three fays, especially Pryl, had overblown the whole topic.

Yawning again, Nari closed her eyes for what seemed like minutes, but was actually several hours. She awoke to howling, but unlike any wolf howls she'd ever heard. A combination of wailing, sniveling, and yowling, the noises sounded not quite wolf-made. A chill ran through her, and she scrambled to her feet, tying her cape more securely around her throat. Taking up her sword, she stepped out of her tent. Pryl was beside her in an instant, joined by Pawllah, Elanya, and her parents. It seemed everyone had slept in their clothes, with their swords at hand.

"Nari, return to your tent," hissed Selden.

Nari shook her head. There was no way she was staying behind, but she couldn't say that to her father, because he would simply order her back to the tent. She wouldn't defy Selden in front of the others. Instead she said, "I'm safer with the rest of you." Selden glanced at Ayala, who nodded grimly.

The six of them filed out of their row and past the servants' tents. Selden's manservant, Korl, hurried to join them, his sword drawn. Selden ordered him to bring around their horses and then stay behind to guard the campsite with the other Tanglewood servants.

They led their horses toward a group of Arrowood clansmen, Mordahn among them, suited up in their chainmail and helms, preparing to mount their horses. Orbahn turned to Ayala and Selden, and waved his hand, his voice tense. "Please, my Liege, return with your clan to the tents. This is Arrowood's problem. We will handle it."

Ayala drew her shoulders back, ready to take on Orbahn. But Nari knew her mother well, understood she had many tactics for handling male chieftains who didn't want her poking her nose where they thought she didn't belong. Ayala's voice was soft yet steely. "Chief Orbahn, as your Liege, I cannot turn my back on you or your clan. If Arrowood has a problem with wolves, my clan is only too happy to assist. We will accompany you." She added that last part in a tone that invited no debate.

Orbahn gave a small bow. "Thank you, Liege Ayala, Chief Selden." Glancing behind them, he nodded at the fays. "You are welcome to join us, of course." He noticed Nari for the first time and drew his brows together. "Lady Tanglewood, I believe you should stay behind. You will be safer here."

Mordahn turned toward Nari. "My father is right. This is a hunt, not a joy ride. Please return to your tent."

Nari's face flushed with anger at both men, but especially Mordahn. *How dare he dismiss me like that, and in front of both our clans?* She was about to object, but Selden interceded. "Our daughter is as skilled with her blade as anyone. And she is the future Faymon Liege. It is time she joins us in battle." Nari wanted to applaud her father's speech, but she knew him well enough to realize he would have preferred for her to stay in the camp, if indeed that were safer. The fact Selden wanted her to remain with him and Ayala, even if they were facing down a pack of ferocious wolves, meant he thought she'd be safer by his side.

Orbahn's face closed down and he nodded curtly. "As you wish." Nari glanced over at Mordahn, who shook his head, scowling. After this was over, she would make sure he understood boundaries. Mordahn would not speak to her so dismissively again, neither publicly nor privately.

They rode in the direction of the eerie howling, urging their horses forward despite their natural reluctance. A bright moon lit the sky overhead, although the tall trees mostly obscured it. Pryl rode with one hand on his reins, the other holding a fireball aloft. The yowling and wailing grew louder, strange wolf yet not-wolf sounds filling the air. Something seemed seriously wrong with this pack.

The trail widened and Pryl pulled alongside Nari. She sensed he had something to say but was either too polite or too shy to voice it. "What's on your mind? Please don't hold back. No one else does."

Pryl exhaled, the flame in his palm flickering. "I do not like how your fiancé addressed you. It was wrong, he was wrong."

Nari glanced at Pryl's profile, his aquiline nose, strong chin, and wavy hair, which seemed to almost glisten in the light of the flame. "Thanks for saying so. I agree—I'll speak to him."

"Words alone will not move a man like him."

"What do you suggest?"

Shouting and yelling interrupted them, and a couple of horses bolted off the trail. They heard several clansmen ahead of them cry, "Grihms! Wolves and grihms!" Wolfish howls and un-wolfish moans filled the air.

"What's a grihm?" hissed Nari, gripping her reins more tightly, the eerie moans making her scalp tingle with fear.

Pryl's jaw tensed. "Wolf-human crossbreed."

Nari gasped. "But crossbreeds are illegal! How can this be?" Not only was crossbreeding outlawed, no mage would ever consent to misusing Serving magic in this way.

Pryl looked at her, his gray eyes solemn. He didn't

need to say anything; he'd been right all along. Nari muttered under her breath, "'Tis Fallow magic." She felt her future tilting out of alignment, her plans and dreams slipping away: the rites of binding, with all five Faymon clans coming together in a weeklong celebration, her beautiful new gown and wardrobe, the longhouse in Arrowood, her broad-shouldered husband. All gone in a breath, in a whisper on the wind, *Fallow magic.*

"On your left!" yelled Pryl, extinguishing his flame and withdrawing his sword in one fluid movement. He shouted a defensive incantation. "Conjure a shield around this spot, defend with strength against onslaught!" Nari incanted the spell with him, but nothing happened.

Pryl frowned in confusion, and Nari saw a flicker of fear in his eyes. As a fay-born mage, not being able to access his magic would be inconceivable to him. Nari reached deep inside, probing for her magic's life force, but she searched in vain. She felt no sparks of magical energy. Her Serving magic—and Pryl's—had been disabled somehow.

Nari's palomino, Goldah, reared as a pair of wolves charged Pryl and Nari. One of the wolves was hideously deformed in the face, with a human forehead and eyes, and wolfish snout and muzzle. The creature had a bushy tail and four wolf legs, with a pair of furry human hands for paws attached to its two front legs.

"Oh my stars," cried Nari, swinging her blade at the wolf-man. He bared his teeth at her and lunged, wrapping his two hand-like paws around her leg and tugging.

Nari lost her balance and toppled off Goldah, who neighed and took off running. Nari didn't blame her.

Nari landed on her side, her sword fallen behind her. The grihm snapped its jaws at her, and something in the way the grihm moved told Nari the crossbreed was newly turned, still retaining some human instincts. Nari pushed herself to a seated position and yelled, "No!" The grihm hesitated a fraction. Nari used her mage's commanding voice and shouted into the trees and the wind: "I am Lady Tanglewood, protector of Serving magic. My clan will stop this wicked sorcery!"

Nari pointed to her mother and Pawllah ahead of her, and her father and Elanya behind her. The lead grihm yowled into the air. The wolves and grihms surrounding the Tanglewood group withdrew six paces, their sides heaving. One of the Arrowood warriors ran up behind the lead grihm and ran him through with his blade. The other wolves attacked the clansman. Nari scrambled to her feet and took up her sword, ready to help, but Pryl placed a hand on her shoulder. "Leave him. It's wolf justice, and in this case it's not wrong."

Nari's stomach turned at the gruesome sight, bile rising in her throat. Turning away, she crouched on the ground and took a series of deep, cleansing breaths. Selden and Ayala dismounted and converged on Nari at the same time. Her father placed a comforting hand on her back.

Nari straightened and turned toward her parents, her eyes moist with unshed tears. Nothing in these woods was what it seemed. She wished she'd never set foot in

Arrowood, never met Orbahn or laid eyes on Mordahn, never saw a grihm, nor what a pack of wolves could do to a man.

"Are you injured?" asked her mother, sounding more anxious than Nari had ever heard her. Ayala pointed at Nari's leather boot, scored with the grihm's teeth marks. Nari shook her head, not yet able to find her voice.

Elanya and Pawllah joined them. A look passed between the fays. Pryl nodded, his face pale in the moonlight. Pawllah's voice was barely a whisper, so quietly did she speak. "Most of the pack are dead or dying, including the escaped crossbreeds. Orbahn and Mordahn are approaching."

"Quickly, let's cast a defensive shield," hissed Ayala. She murmured the same incantation that Pryl and Nari had tried earlier, but as before, their magic was silent, deadened to their summoning. "What's going on?" asked Ayala, her face pinched with worry. "Serving magic has never failed us."

This made no sense to Nari. Even surrounded by Fallow magic on all sides, they should have no trouble calling upon Serving magic. Something else was causing the blockage. Then Nari remembered the medicinal taste in her mouth the previous evening. "The wine from last night. Did you drink any?" she asked. Everyone nodded, although Elanya wrinkled her nose. "It was not to my liking, but I drank a little to be polite. Why?"

"Mine had an odd aftertaste, almost metallic. Could someone have tampered with our drinks?" asked Nari.

Pryl stared at her. "Twisted steel, ground to a very fine powder."

"Even a small amount would render our magic useless," said Ayala grimly. Twisted steel was comprised mostly of iron, which counteracted magic, plus traces of carbon and fay gold to strengthen its properties. Mages convicted of crimes were bound with twisted steel manacles to ensure they didn't get up to any magical mischief while incarcerated.

"We'll be without our magic for a day at least, perhaps longer, depending on the amount ingested," grunted Pryl.

Orbahn reached their group first, Arrowood clansmen on either side of him. Mordahn stood behind his father, his eyes downcast. *He can no longer deny what his father is,* thought Nari.

"I am relieved to see you and your clan are unharmed." Orbahn gave Ayala and Selden a stiff bow. "Although the elder fay appears unwell." He nodded at Elanya, who was heaving into the thick undergrowth on the opposite side of the road. The fay's loud retching sounds made Nari feel queasy. She wondered how much wine Elanya had ingested the previous evening, despite her claims to have sampled the beverage out of politeness. Pawllah generally enjoyed two or three mugs of wine with every meal.

Ayala raised a finger and pointed at Orbahn. Her voice shook with barely suppressed rage. "Chief Orbahn, the forests of Arrowood reek with your Fallow sorcery. I've seen your crossbreeds and swallowed your contaminated wine." She spat on the ground. "When I return to Tanglewood, I will call an emergency meeting of the other clans. The council will decide how to deal with you."

Selden moved next to Ayala, so they stood shoulder to shoulder. "There will be no rites of binding," he growled. "No daughter of Tanglewood will ever wed a son of Arrowood."

Orbahn curled his lip, sneering, "I believe you are mistaken, Chief Selden. My son will wed your impudent daughter. The little Liege will learn to obey her husband's commands."

Selden thrust out his jaw, his hand on the hilt of his sword. "Over my dead body."

"I'm sorry you feel that way." Orbahn grunted and reached into his belt, withdrawing a dagger. He flung it, the tip of the blade piercing Selden's throat. Selden clutched his neck, falling onto the hard-packed soil.

"Father!" cried Nari, throwing herself onto the ground next to him.

Ayala screamed Selden's name and charged Orbahn, her sword in her right hand, dagger in her left. Pawllah, Pryl, and Elanya, who'd stopped heaving by then, took up their swords against the Arrowood clansmen who were advancing on them.

Nari heard Mordahn holler at Orbahn, "Father, what have you done?" She was dimly aware that Mordahn took up arms against her clan, although in his case it was self-defense, since the fays left him little choice. The sounds of swords swishing, blades clanging, and clansmen shouting filled the forest.

Selden's lips moved. Nari gripped his hand, sobbing. She leaned over to hear her father as he gurgled a single word, "Run." Selden's eyes flickered and he was gone. Sobbing harder, Nari gently closed his eyes. She brushed the hair back from his face and placed a kiss on his forehead. As Selden's spirit was released, so too was his magic. Nari closed her eyes and concentrated on sensing Selden's magical energy. By catching and indwelling several of his passing sparks, she was paying homage to him as a Serving mage.

Tears streaming down her face, Nari rose on shaking legs. Most of the Arrowood clansmen were dead or dying, either from the earlier grihm attack or from fay blades. Mordahn was on his knees, his hands raised in surrender. Pawllah stood behind him, the tip of her blade pressed against Mordahn's back.

Elanya was also on her knees, leaning over Pryl lying still on the ground. Nari's stomach clenched and she cried out, "Pryl!" She picked up her sword and started toward him, but Ayala and Orbahn blocked her path, the two of them locked in a tight fighting circle. Ayala clearly had the upper hand. Orbahn's chest heaved, and his face had gone purple from the exertion.

Ayala pointed her sword at Orbahn. "Surrender now, and I'll spare your life."

Orbahn threw back his head and cackled. Once a respected leader and chieftain, he'd become crazed with Fallow magic and its promise of unbridled power.

Bellowing into the night sky, he called down a curse upon Ayala, freezing her in place. She stood, her arm raised, her sword pointed at Orbahn, unable to take one more step forward. Orbahn's sorcery had turned Ayala into a statue so brittle her breath froze on her lips.

Nari pivoted toward Ayala, the adrenaline pumping through her body, all her focus on saving her mother. She had the briefest of moments, the span of two dozen breaths, to defend her mother against Orbahn's blade and break his spell. Otherwise, Ayala would die, rooted in place, out of oxygen and out of time.

Nari charged toward Orbahn, screaming "Evakunouz!" an ancient fay war cry she'd read in one of Pawllah's old scrolls. It translated roughly as "retreat or die," although Pawllah had explained that in the old tongue, it actually meant "drop to the ground and bow before me, or I shall boil your entrails in your own blood." At the time, Nari had shuddered at the vivid imagery, finding it hard to believe someone could hate another so much as to invoke such language.

With a wave of his hand, Orbahn sent Nari tumbling to the ground, her legs caving beneath her. His Fallow spell knocked the wind from her lungs and she gasped for air, knowing as she did so, her mother was gasping inside the prison of her own body. Nari gritted her teeth, pushing against the Fallow spell Orbahn had hurled at her. She hauled herself to her feet, and grabbing her sword from the ground, charged Orbahn again.

Orbahn glanced her way, surprise flickering across his face. "Enough! There will be no more Tanglewood

Lieges!" With one fluid motion, he plunged his blade into Ayala's chest, breaking the spell that bound her in place. Ayala dropped to the unyielding soil. Nari flung herself on top of her mother's lifeless form. A keening rose from the forest floor, shattering Nari's heart with the rawness of its grief. She started to raise her hands, to block the lament from her ears, until she realized the wailing came from her own lips.

"No, no! Mama, please don't leave me!" Nari's words caught in her throat as she heard someone—was it Orbahn?—yowl like a stuck pig and then a thud as another body fell onto the road. Hands clutched Nari's shoulders and tried pulling her away from Ayala's body. Familiar hands, the same hands that had rapped Nari's knuckles when she'd misbehaved as a young girl, and later, showed Nari how to brew a potion or mend a broken pot. *Could these hands save Ayala now?*

Nari gripped Pawllah's hands, pulling her down next to her and begging, "Please, do something. I can't lose her too."

Pawllah knelt beside Nari and shook her head sadly. "Your mother is gone, lass. Our Lady Liege is dead. All you can do now is catch some of her magic before the sparks have entirely dispersed."

"No!" screamed Nari, the darkness of the trees and the night, of Arrowood itself, pressing in on her. A tiny voice, barely a sigh, curled around her, murmuring in her ear, reminding her there was yet another way. "You can bring her back if you want. You've studied the old scrolls. You know it can be done."

Pawllah yanked her hands from Nari's as if she'd been burned, and scrambled to her feet. She spat on the ground by Nari's boots, her eyes glittering coldly. "Just this once, because of what happened here tonight, I will forgive you. But if I ever hear you suggesting the dark ways again, I will turn my back on you, and so will all the fays. You will be utterly cut off and alone."

Nari brought her hands up to her face, blood and dirt mixing with her tears. "I'm sorry," she whispered, ashamed of herself, of what she'd suggested. "So very sorry." She was now the Liege, or would be soon, following the crowning ceremony. Nari would be sworn to protect Serving magic, but in her grief and brokenness, she'd suggested necromancy. Nari knew Pawllah was speaking the truth. Her fay tutor would forgive her this one time, and they'd never discuss it again. She doubted Elanya would have been so understanding.

Nari sensed her mother's magic glimmering nearby, as if waiting for Nari to indwell some of it. Nari captured what she could of the stray sparks and sobbed as she felt Ayala's remaining magic dissipating.

Elanya ran over to them, her own face tear stained. "Oh, my dear Ayala, and Selden too." She shook her head and let out a shaky breath. "We must move quickly. Young Pryl needs a fay healer, right away."

Pawllah's head snapped up. "But how? I'm unable to access my magic even now. I still have too much twisted steel running through my veins."

"I had very little to drink last night." Elanya pointed to the side of the road where she'd been retching. "I expelled enough of the tainted wine so I could sense my magic again. Although it is dulled, I will be able to transport Pryl home. But I'll not be able to carry the rest of you with me."

Pawllah waved her hand. "Go now, save Pryl. Nari and I will travel by horseback."

Elanya nodded solemnly and returning to Pryl's side, gripped his hand. Foggy tendrils groped along the ground and curled around Pryl and the elder fay. The vapors swirled around them, enveloping them in Elanya's traveling mists. When the fog cleared, Pryl and Elanya were gone.

Nari stood up, her legs as shaky as her insides. Orbahn had fallen nearby, a bloom of red spreading across his back. "Who slew Orbahn?"

Pawllah set her mouth in a firm line. "I did. I only wish I'd done it sooner, before all this." She spread out her arms at the bodies littering the ground.

Nari remembered Mordahn and saw him lying on his side. Her heart thudded in her chest at his passing —far too young—but also at what might have been, at the heat of his kisses, at the hopes they'd shared together. Nari raised her hand, pointing. "And Mordahn too?"

Pawllah shook her head. "I knocked him out. Mordahn has not chosen his path yet. I'll not kill an innocent man."

Relief flooded through Nari and she swayed slightly. She no longer wanted to marry Mordahn, but she didn't want to see him dead either. She'd witnessed enough bloodshed that night. "But what if he chooses the wrong path?"

"Then you and I will stop him, but not before. Serving magic demands justice, not vengeance. This is the true path."

Nari repeated the phrase, used by fays to acknowledge the Serving way. "This is the true path." She added, "I'm glad he's not dead."

"Let us hope you will not come to regret those words."

Nari shrugged. She had enough to deal with right now, without worrying about how Mordahn would live his life in some distant future. All she knew for certain was she would not be joining him at the Arrowood longhouse he'd built for them. She never wanted to set foot in his clan's cursed forests again. "We need to move my parents. I don't want to hold their funeral rites on Arrowood land."

"Aye, lass," murmured Pawllah. "We must care for our dead. And then we will see what comes of all this spilt blood."

Nari scanned the road and spotted their horses, cowering some distance away. She whistled. Goldah approached, the other horses following behind. Goldah tossed her head and snorted through her nostrils. Nari figured her sweet palomino wanted to be anywhere but on the dark Arrowood road, in the aftermath of battle, the tang of blood and sweat filling the air. She spoke quietly, patting Goldah's neck, and then moved on to Beulah, her mother's gentle mare. After rubbing her hands down her neck and quivering body, Nari picked up Beulah's reins and tugged. "Come, we have work to do."

Pawllah and Nari rode side by side, guiding the horses carrying Selden and Ayala behind them. As they approached the Arrowood campsite, Korl stepped out of the shadows. "My master!" he cried out when he saw Selden's body draped over his stallion. Another cry escaped his lips. "And my Liege!"

Korl peered behind their horses. "Who did this? Tell me. I promise to repay their murders, blood for blood."

"Orbahn slew them both. He is dead, by my hand," said Pawllah. "Why are you on the road, and not at the tents with the others?"

"I heard horses and ran here to see who approached." Korl shook his head as tears leaked down his lined face. "Everyone else is dead. Slain in their tents."

"What?" cried Nari, the news of more deaths cutting through her numbness. These were more than servants to her. They were clansmen and friends. They had laughed together, and they would have mourned together over Ayala and Selden. Nari's chest ached at the fresh loss. "Tell us, quickly."

Korl sniffled a few times, wiping his face on his sleeve. He took a deep breath. "Something spooked our horses. They were raising a mighty ruckus, and so I went to check on them. I was worried about the wolves and stayed with the horses, in case the pack showed up here. Then I heard a scream and ran back to find the other servants dead, by Arrowood's hand."

"How many?" Nari asked, hoping she'd not have to

fight any more Arrowood clansmen before she laid her parents to rest. "And where are those murderers now?"

Korl's large hands rested on the hilts of his swords, one on each hip. "Three, and they did not escape my blades." He raised his deeply etched face to Nari. "What now, my Liege?"

Nari furrowed her brow, confused by Korl's question. Why was Korl looking at her, but asking her mother for direction? The Liege was dead.

Pawllah came to her rescue. "Liege Nari does not want to build her parents' funeral pyres on Arrowood land."

Oh my stars, thought Nari, *I've inherited Mother's title. And her responsibilities, including dealing with the Arrowood clan.* Then it struck her; Mordahn was now the Chief of Arrowood. She shook her head at the terrible turn of events that put her and Mordahn on opposing sides, clan against clan, Serving magic against Fallow sorcery. Even if Mordahn himself had not dabbled in it, he would have known, should have known, what Orbahn was doing. He must have seen the grihms his father had been breeding. Something so barbarous can't be kept hidden for long.

Nari knew what she had to do next: lay her parents to rest. Everything else, all the fallout from their murders and Orbahn's betrayal would have to wait. They had more than a half-day's ride to clear Arrowood, and then another couple of days' ride through Riverwood territory before reaching Tanglewood's outer boundary—if they rode at a normal pace, which they could not.

No, she had to find a safe place to set up her parents'

funeral bier, and it would have to be on Riverwood land, not Tanglewood. While Riverwood had sworn allegiance to Liege Ayala more than twenty years earlier, Nari knew her mother often grumbled about Riverwood always siding with Arrowood during council meetings. Nari would need to be very careful while in Riverwood, and hope that word of what happened did not travel far, at least until she could send her parents properly to the realms of the dead.

Nari compressed her mouth into a straight line, a plan forming in her mind. "We need to keep moving. Given our slow pace, I doubt we'll be out of Arrowood territory until well after sunrise. Once we set foot in Riverwood, I want to find a safe place to set up my parents' bier. We will hold their funeral rites immediately. I know this is by no means customary, but we have no choice. We are a clan on the run at the moment."

She looked at her father's loyal manservant. "Korl, run ahead, back to the camp. Grab our saddlebags, and anything my father or mother wouldn't want to fall into Arrowood hands. Leave the tents and everything else. We'll meet you at the far edge of the campsite. Oh, and don't forget to take the pigeons. We'll need them later."

Faymons used carrier pigeons to relay messages between families and clans. Ayala never traveled far without her pigeons, a precaution that Nari was grateful for at the moment. Then Nari remembered Pryl at the campfire last night, his deep, soothing baritone, his fingers delicately plucking the stringed instrument in his lap. "And Pryl's lyre, please retrieve that as well."

Korl bowed from the waist. "Aye, my Liege. As you wish." He turned and sprinted down the road.

"Tell me what you are thinking," said Pawllah quietly.

Nari sighed. "I expect Arrowood will take up arms against us, even though Orbahn murdered my parents. I want to reach our stronghold before that happens."

"You believe Mordahn will turn against you?"

Nari met Pawllah's piercing eyes. Her fay tutor missed nothing. "His clan has already turned against us. Mordahn was wearing battledress when he greeted me, although I don't believe he had an inkling Orbahn would kill my parents. But when Mordahn receives my message, he will have no illusions this can be patched up."

"What message is that?"

"Calling off the rites of binding, of course."

"And?" prompted Pawllah. Her tutor knew her well. Nari would not stop there, not given what had happened, the betrayal of her clan, the murder of her parents.

Nari spoke with a firmness that belied her raw emotional state. "And informing Mordahn that the Arrowood clan will be brought before the council on charges of treason. His clan will be stripped of its voting rights until they've proven their allegiance, which will take a very long time. Further, all practitioners of Fallow sorcery will be banished. They will become outcasts among the clans."

"You are right, of course. But you do realize where this will lead?"

Nari nodded, her throat tight with grief for her parents and fury at Orbahn and his clan. "There will be war, clan against clan. And more Fallow sorcery for us to root out before this is over."

"We are Serving mages. This is the true path."

"Aye," Nari exhaled, her breath bitter, tainted by poisoned wine and fresh betrayal. "This is the true path."

CHAPTER

FLIGHT

NARI

OTHER THAN A STARTLED DOE AND TWO FAWNS, WHICH scurried away at the sound of their horses' hooves, they encountered no one else. The day broke clear and warm, although not overly hot. Wild lilac and lilies grew along the road, scenting the air with their fragrance. Goldfinches, robins, and chickadees trilled to one another from the tall oaks and maples. Nari scowled at the perfect spring morning, the sunshine and flowers and birds with their cheerful chirping. Her parents, the mighty warrior, Chief Selden, and the wise and powerful Liege Ayala, were dead. And yet the woods gave no notice of their passing, as if their lives and deaths had been nothing more than an inkblot in the scrolls of history.

"We've crossed into Riverwood," said Pawllah. Nari sensed it too, the fragrant air less cloying, the sun shining more brightly, as if someone had drawn back a heavy curtain.

Nari called out to Korl, "You know these woods better than anyone. Can you find us a quiet spot for the funeral rites?"

"Aye, I've been thinking about little else. I know a good place not far from here."

Nari waved her hand. "The sooner we can do this for my parents, the better."

Pawllah agreed. "The daylight gives us some advantage, particularly since I still can't cast a proper spell to shield us from view. The flames from the funeral pyre will be less noticeable now than at night."

Korl led them off the road, along a creek bed still swollen with the spring rains. They clopped along slowly, avoiding the worst of the mud, until they reached a widening of the creek. Nari dismounted and quickly surveyed the area Korl had found. They were well shielded from the road, had plenty of wood to build the bier, and access to water for cleansing the bodies, as well as dousing the ashes when they finished. As Nari ticked off each of the items needed for her parents' funeral rites, her heart fractured a bit more. She yearned to turn back the wheel of time and prevent her parents from traveling into Arrowood in the first place.

The three of them worked quickly, all the while keeping a sharp eye for any riders from Arrowood. Korl built the bier, while Pawllah and Nari prepared the bodies. They cleansed Ayala and Selden's wounds and used their capes for burial garments. Under different circumstances, Nari and Pawllah would wrap a clean shroud around each body, tucking fragrant spices into every fold of the shroud, and then drape richly embroidered blankets over each of them. The entire stronghold would have attended Ayala and Selden's funeral rites, as well as the chiefs of the other clans, and their many friends across Faynwood. Tanglewood musicians would have played their pipes and drums as the funeral pyre was lit, the men chanting in rhythm to the drumbeat, the women trilling in reply.

Instead, Nari had to hide in the woods of an indifferent clan and conduct her parents' funeral as if they were the criminals, and not Orbahn and his clansmen. Nari knew if she dwelt too much on the injustice, she'd easily slide toward the need for vengeance. She could feel herself slipping into a dark place at times, as she watched Korl lay her parents' bodies on top of the bier.

"My Liege," said Korl softly, "what should I do about the banner and ribbons?"

Nari frowned, not sure what he was asking. Pawllah nodded. "Good thinking, Korl. Since we're trying to travel without drawing attention to our clan, we should destroy the Tanglewood banner and remove the ribbons from the horses' manes." Korl quickly unwound the purple and gold ribbons from Ayala and Selden's horses, and from Nari's palomino, and laid them on the bier. Last, he pulled down the Tanglewood banner, which he carried in a holster attached to his saddle, and draped the banner on top of Ayala and Selden. The removal of the Tanglewood colors hit Nari hard. She pressed her hand to her chest, pushing against the fresh ache.

Korl turned and waited for a signal from Nari to light the kindling. Nari stumbled over to the bier, tears streaming down her face. Placing a hand on each of her parents, she cried out, "Liege Ayala Elspeth Arlyss and Chief Selden Reye Arlyss, both gone, wrenched from this life too soon! Faynwood's bright morning stars, fallen but never forgotten! Oh Mother and Father, how can this be?" Breaking down completely, her voice a shaky whisper, she offered up a prayer for their souls' safe passage through the realms of the dead.

Nari nodded at Korl and staggered toward Pawllah, who reached over to grip her hand. They watched as the kindling beneath the bier caught the flame, and wept together. Memories of happier times pierced Nari's heart: her father presenting her with Goldah when she turned twelve; her mother imitating a tipsy tribal chieftain; her parents trying not to laugh when Nari drenched everyone, even the judges, during her first magic trial. Nari wanted to curl up somewhere for a week to remember, and to cry, with her mastiff Quel nearby, and pots of tea to carry her through.

She stared at the bier as the flames burned all the way down, until nothing was left but ashes and dust. Korl used a cooking pot, which he filled with water from the creek, to douse any remaining embers. While he worked, Nari pulled two thin slips of parchment, a bottle of purple ink, and a quill from her saddlebag. She quickly penned the most difficult note she'd ever written, which she addressed to her mother's brother, Erick: "Mother and Father are dead, at the hands of Chief Orbahn. Fallow sorcery and betrayals abound in Arrowood. I am safe, traveling with Pawllah and Korl. With a broken heart, Nari Ayala Arlyss of Tanglewood."

Pawllah went to the cages and pulled out the first pigeon, which normally lived in the aviary in Ayala's garden. Nari rolled up the parchment and slipped it into a tiny canister on the bird's leg. She gave him a crust of bread and Pawllah set the pigeon free. Erick and the rest of the stronghold would learn of Orbahn's treachery soon enough.

Nari wrote a second note, which she addressed to Mordahn: "I herewith cancel our rites of binding and break all personal ties with you. The Arrowood clan will be brought before the council on charges of treason." She and Pawllah attached the thin slip of parchment to the second pigeon, which made its home in Arrowood. The bird would fly true, and Mordahn would have no doubt as to Nari's intentions.

They wound their way back to the main road, stopping only to water the horses. They encountered little traffic on the road: a farmer, driving his cows to another pasture, and a troupe of traveling performers, calling out a cheerful greeting as they passed. Toward dusk, they came upon the crossroads that traversed the invisible ley lines running through their land. If they continued straight, they would eventually reach their stronghold; the road to the left would take them to the north woods of Tanglewood and beyond, all the way to Ridgewood, the northernmost boundary of their land; the road to the right would meander southeast and eventually lead them to the Shorewood clan, which guarded the shores of the Pale Sea.

Korl, the first to hear hooves pounding the road behind them, shouted, "Arrowood, coming fast upon us!" The three of them scattered into the woods with their horses, all heading in a different direction in search of a place to hide.

Nari led Goldah into a dense thicket of hawthorn trees lining the side of the road, trying to avoid the two-inch-long thorns. She held onto the reins of Beulah, her mother's mare, but the horse managed to get stuck between two of the hawthorns, and stubbornly refused to budge. Sighing, Nari dismounted. Her hands worked to untangle the mare from the tree branches that had trapped her.

One of the horses on the road slowed down, and something stirred within Nari, unsettling her. She knew without seeing him that Mordahn stood on the other side of the thicket. She performed a quick mental calculation, realizing he must have received her message and immediately ridden after her, with what sounded like half a dozen clansmen alongside him. The woods where her parents had been killed were a couple hours' ride to the Arrowood stronghold. If he'd come this far, this quickly, then Mordahn would have left Arrowood right after reading the message, well before Orbahn's funeral rites, and before his own chieftain's ceremony.

Is Mordahn seeking revenge for his father's death? Or

coming after me, to force me into marriage? Both thoughts filled her with dread, but the idea of being forced into the rites of binding scared her more.

Mordahn dismounted and began to approach the hawthorn trees. Nari could feel his magic probing the woods for her. She froze, her heart pounding so hard she feared he would hear her through the trees. Nari reached into her magic, which still slumbered under the effects of the wine. Closing her eyes, she focused on the simplest spell she could muster and incanted the words, her lips moving silently. "Drape us in a veil of gauze, hide us from inquiring eyes." A veil of drabness unfurled over Nari and the horses, covering them in a gauzy gray film, making it nearly impossible to see them. It wasn't precisely an invisibility spell, since no one could make themselves truly invisible, but a cloaking spell, one that mages' children learned early, since it was considered the most basic of the defensive spells.

Mordahn stood there a bit longer, scanning the trees. Nari poured all her energy into maintaining the veil, repeating the words of the spell on a continuous loop. Her head started to throb with the effort, since her magic was still lethargic. Finally, she heard Mordahn's boots retreating back to his horse. He mounted and was off again, galloping toward Eloway, the Liege's stronghold inside Tanglewood. Nari doubted whether Mordahn would ride all the way to Eloway, before doubling back to search for her. She heaved a deep sigh at the thought of Eloway, realizing she'd not be able to return to her clan's enclave, at least not anytime soon, not with Mordahn prowling the main road.

"Nari," hissed Pawllah, "where are you?"

Nari dropped the veil of drabness and clutched her head, suddenly dizzy. "Over here," she whispered. Pawllah found her leaning against a hawthorn tree. Goldah whickered nearby, as if relieved Mordahn was gone.

Pawllah finished untangling Beulah from the thicket. "I confess my heart was in my throat when Mordahn dismounted and stared into the woods after you. But I couldn't summon my magic to help you." The fay peered at Nari more closely. "Are you unwell?"

Nari guided Goldah away from the hawthorn trees. "I managed to cast a veil of drabness, but it's drained me."

Pawllah arched her eyebrows. "Well, at least one of us can cast a child's spell. That's something anyway."

Nari tilted her head. "Just how much wine did you drink the other night?"

Pawllah sniffed, ignoring her question. Korl joined them and pointed in the direction Mordahn had ridden. "Mordahn will discover soon enough he's lost our trail. I don't think it's safe to continue on the main road."

"Aye." Nari nodded. "I'm thinking we need to find a way to divert Mordahn's attention."

"What do you have in mind?" asked Pawllah.

Nari didn't see how they could make it to Eloway with Mordahn pursuing her. Regardless of what he intended to do when or if he caught up with her, Nari decided that avoidance was the better strategy. Despite all that had happened, she didn't want to raise a sword against him. Mordahn had always looked up to his father, and he would be hurting now too, which meant he wasn't thinking as rationally as he ought. "We let Mordahn believe we've ridden to condcle with my father's family in the north, rather than heading directly to our stronghold in Eloway."

"How?" asked Pawllah.

Nari patted Beulah. She'd miss this connection to her mother, but she didn't see another way. "We take my cape, stuff it to look as if I'm inside it, and strap it on top of Mother's horse. We do the same with your cape, Pawllah, and my father's stallion. Then Korl takes the horses on the road to the north woods. He'll pass by several villages on the way, getting just close enough so they can see three riders."

Korl scratched his beard. "It might work, especially after nightfall. It would give you some time to escape, but where would you go?"

"Southeast to Shorewood, and all the way to the Pale Sea if need be," said Nari.

Pawllah scrunched up her face, thinking. "It's as good a plan as any, especially without my magic to help us."

They worked fast, creating two effigies to set on top of her parents' horses. Nari kissed each horse goodbye, swallowing hard against the lump in her throat. Korl bowed low before he mounted and recited the Serving mage's blessing, "May your magic serve in peace and lead through service, my Liege."

Nari repeated the blessing, and then Korl was off, riding fast toward the north. She and Pawllah turned their horses around. Nari wore a burgundy riding jacket against the evening chill. She had stuffed her long hair into a peaked cap of her father's, which he used to wear on his morning walks with the dogs back home, pipe in hand. The lingering scent of her father's tobacco brought back fresh memories of Selden, Ayala, and all she'd lost.

They rode through the night, Nari struggling at times to remain upright on Goldah's back. She nearly slipped from her saddle twice, exhausted from lack of sleep and the strain of using magic despite ingesting twisted steel. When the first blue bands of light appeared in the sky, Pawllah said, "Lass, you need some rest. We both do. Let's look for somewhere to bunk down and rest the horses."

Nari yawned. "Aye. Besides, I'd rather not be traveling in the open during the day."

Pawllah canted her head to the right. "We'll have better luck over here. I sense a snug cave tucked into those bluffs."

Fays had remarkable geolocation instincts, in addition to their keen ability to read faces, moods, and sometimes, minds. Once, while preparing for the junior magic trials when she was eleven, Nari had crept into Pawllah's study and "borrowed" an advanced spell book. She'd hoped to find a spell so powerful she could ace the trials. When confronted about the missing book, Nari had lied, her untruths spiraling into a fanciful story, one lie leading to another. Her fay tutor saw through her immediately, unraveling the lies and Nari's motives, which boiled down to the fear of failing in front of her parents and clan. Nari was furious. In her anger, she accused Pawllah of being a mind reader, and her tutor had rapped her knuckles with a wooden rod. Nari later learned that publicly accusing a fay of being a mind reader was a major insult, akin to leveraging a charge of oath breaking.

After that incident, Nari never mentioned mind reading again, but sometimes she detected Elanya or Pawllah, their faces blank, psychically zeroing in on an ambassador or council member from another clan. She suspected they were doing nothing more than gently probing inside the visitor's head, trying to suss out motives and prevent any harm coming to Tanglewood. Nari only wished they could have been more effective with Chief Orbahn, but his Fallow sorcery may have been sufficient to mask his true intentions.

Pawllah's inerrant sense of direction eventually guided them to the snug cave she'd promised. Nari slid off Goldah and placed a hand against the horse's flank to steady herself. She began removing the palomino's saddle, but Pawllah waved her off. "You look ready to keel over. Go lie down. I'll see to the horses." She paused, adding, "My magic is still sluggish, but I can feel it start to flow again. I'll be able to cast enough protective wards around us to throw Mordahn off our scent."

Nari stumbled into the cave, threw her bedroll on the ground, and crawled inside. She woke suddenly, her pulse pounding, hours later. The cave smelled of blackberry wine, Pawllah's favorite, which the fay must have stashed away in her saddlebags the week before, at the start of their journey to Orbahn's stronghold. Based on the loud snores emanating from the bedroll nearby, the fay tutor had imbibed quite a bit before falling asleep.

Nari heard a thump outside the cave and bolted upright, the back of her neck prickling. She used her magic to probe for the shielding wards Pawllah had cast before turning in; they were down, which meant something or someone had gotten through. Nari tried to cast a quick protective ward but nothing happened. She felt panicky and tried again. She couldn't even summon a veil of drabness. Something was very wrong. Nari pulled on her boots and felt for her sword, lying on the ground next to her. She grasped the hilt and stepped around Pawllah's sleeping form.

Creeping to the mouth of the cave, she paused to allow her eyes to adjust. A golden patch of sunlight lit the ground beyond the entrance. Nari had no idea how long she'd slept, but it felt like late afternoon. A twig snapped, followed by the sound of boots crunching through the undergrowth. Nari tried to calm her stuttering heart. She slipped outside the cave, her sword raised, her legs quivering.

"Lower your sword, Nari. I've come to talk with you, not fight." Mordahn stood beneath a copse of oak trees, his face in shadow. A crumpled form in a silver cape lay curled at his feet.

NARI

Nari panicked, convinced Pryl had come searching for her, but instead found Mordahn's knife in his back. She brought her hand to her throat, grief threatening to overwhelm her. She took a few steps closer, her sword still raised in her right hand, and then spotted a tightly coiled blue bun sticking out of the hood of the cape. "Elanya!" cried Nari, relief flooding through her that Pryl hadn't fallen to Mordahn's knife, followed by guilt at her feelings for Pryl, and sorrow for the elder fay. Elanya's only crime had been her loyalty to Tanglewood. Nari's voice shook. "What have you done to her?"

"That fay woman killed my father." Mordahn shrugged. "I didn't think to be able to avenge his death so soon, but that's not the reason I've come."

Great stars, he thinks Elanya killed Orbahn. Nari thought back to that horrific scene on the road to

Arrowood. Elanya standing near Pryl, who'd been injured. Pawllah behind Mordahn, her sword in his back. Pawllah had knocked Mordahn unconscious and then ran Orbahn through with her sword. However, Elanya and Pawllah were the same height and distinctly fay, with their vivid blue hair and shimmery silver capes. Mordahn would have questioned any of the Arrowood survivors and learned a fay woman had killed Orbahn. He happened to choose the wrong fay woman for his revenge.

Nari gripped her sword more firmly. "I don't understand. How did you even get here?"

Mordahn used his toe to nudge Elanya. "I hitched a ride on this one's traveling mists. Caught her off guard. As soon as our feet touched solid ground again, I slit her throat. "

Nari frowned. The last she'd seen of Elanya, the woman was taking Pryl to a fay healer. "How could you have traveled on her mists?"

Mordahn waved his hand impatiently. "Lower your sword, and I'll tell you."

Nari shook her head. "Tell me, and I'll consider lowering my sword."

"Very well," sighed Mordahn, as if he were somehow the injured party. "When I lost your trail on the road to Eloway, I wound up following the manservant with the effigies on top of the horses. Quite a good ruse. Whose idea was that, by the way?"

"Mine."

"Impressive little sneak, aren't you?" Mordahn

snorted and took a few steps toward her. Nari narrowed her eyes at him and pointed with her sword. "Stop right there. Finish what you were saying and then be on your way."

He put his hands up in the air. "Fine. I was furious when I realized I'd lost you again, and then the fay woman showed up on her traveling mists. Naturally, I crept closer to listen. The manservant explained you were heading for Shorewood. The fay woman seemed to waver a bit, as if she were probing for you, and then she said, 'Aye, I've found them. Pawllah's cast a clumsy spell, her magic's still not right.' I'll confess, my hopes went up. I was determined to follow that murderous fay. When those traveling vapors wrapped around her legs, I ran right into the mists. And here I am." He spread his arms wide, as if to embrace Nari, and stepped forward. They were little more than eight feet apart.

"Not one step closer. I mean it." Nari tried backing away, but her foot hit the solid rock of the cave. She didn't want Mordahn to know Pawllah was inside and so sidestepped away from the entrance. "You still haven't told me why you've come."

"To discuss this." He withdrew her hastily scrawled note and threw it on the ground.

"What's there to discuss? Your father killed my parents."

Mordahn bowed his head. "I'm sorry, Nari. My father was wrong, very wrong. But I'm not my father. You have to believe me. I'd never hurt you."

"But you must have known, must have seen what he

was doing. Those poor crossbreeds." Nari shuddered, and her sword arm wavered.

Mordahn leapt across the distance between them, tackling her to the ground. He wrenched the sword from her hand and flung it away. She cried out as Mordahn gripped both her arms, using his body weight to pin her down. She tried shifting underneath him but she couldn't move. She gasped, "You're crushing me. Get off!"

Mordahn was in no hurry to move. She remembered what Pryl had said, about Mordahn needing to choose between darkness and light, between Fallow sorcery or Serving magic. Nari sensed him vacillating, uncertain of himself and his path. He stared down at her, and she saw something dark flit behind his eyes. Nari struggled beneath him, her pulse pounding. Her lungs burned as fury mixed with fear within her. Her eyes fluttered open and closed, and she began to drift, dizzy with lack of oxygen. He was literally crushing her, his much larger body flattening hers. She thought about what Mordahn might do to her if she blacked out entirely and pleaded, "I can't breathe. Please."

Mordahn waited three or four beats before shifting just enough so Nari could gulp in some air. His powerful arms held her in place, and his legs draped across hers. Nari struggled and he tightened his grip again, so she went slack. Nari tried to summon her magic, but as before, nothing happened. Then it dawned on her that Mordahn must have cast a spell to freeze all magic in place. Such spells were temporary and eventually wore off. However, for now, she was defenseless. No magic and no sword. All she had left were her wits.

"If we're going to talk, can we at least sit up?"

A muscle ticked beneath Mordahn's left eye. He seemed to be having some internal struggle. Finally he nodded, rolling off her completely. He stood up, pulling her up and half dragging her to a boulder. "Have a seat." Nari didn't have much choice. She sat down, her knees shaking badly. Mordahn chose to stand, towering over her, blocking the slanting rays of the sun. *It will be dusk soon*, she thought, *and then what?*

"You said you'd never hurt me."

"Aye, and I won't."

"But you just did. You scared me and hurt me."

Mordahn raked a hand through his hair. "I didn't mean to...I just couldn't get you to listen."

"I'm listening now. Say what you've come to say." *And then leave me alone because I never want to see you again.* Nari bit off the rest of her sentence, knowing it would just antagonize him further.

Mordahn sat down next to her on the boulder, his shoulder brushing hers. He picked up one of her hands, threading his fingers through hers. Nari suppressed the urge to recoil from his touch. She needed to be smart, bide her time. She took several calming breaths and waited.

"You're right about the crossbreeds. I found out and confronted my father, but he assured me his breeding program was merely a scientific experiment, nothing more."

"But it's illegal and unethical. Plus, he used Fallow sorcery to perform the crossbreeding, which is also illegal. That's two strikes against your father, right there. And then my parents—" Nari broke off but forced herself to continue. "Your father murdered my parents."

"And now my father lies dead, by your clan."

Nari whipped her head around, glaring at Mordahn. "Your father's death was just; my parents' deaths were not. Don't ever, ever think you can equate the two."

Mordahn stared down at his boots, refusing to meet her eyes. Ignoring her last comment, he pointed at the piece of parchment on the ground. "Your note, the coldness in your words, pierced me to the core. I confess I went a little crazy. I'd already lost my father and many friends on the Arrowood road. I couldn't imagine losing you too. I left my stronghold immediately, before the funeral rites for my father and clansmen. Doesn't that give you some idea of how I feel about you?"

Nari refused to coddle him any longer. "It shows me only that you are possessive," she said fiercely. "And I am not a possession you can chase after like some prey."

"Don't be ridiculous. I don't think of you as prey, you silly girl. You're a prize—my betrothed, the new Faymon Liege—who will rule from Arrowood, and not Tanglewood."

Orbahn's manipulations suddenly fell into place. The clan chief wanted his son to wed the future Liege in order to shift the balance of power among the clans, from Tanglewood to Arrowood. Nari didn't think Orbahn had planned to kill her parents on the Arrowood road, but he would have gotten around to it eventually, well after the rites of binding. He would have chosen poison, if the tainted wine were any indication, and they likely would have died at different times, so as not to cast any suspicions his way. But Orbahn's ultimate goal had been to cut Nari off from her own clan and family; her only refuge would have been her husband, and Arrowood.

Nari vibrated with anger. She felt the stirring of her magic deep within her, whatever spell Mordahn had cast slinking away from her. She'd always been the more gifted mage, his spells no match for what she could do when she summoned her full power. A memory came to her, her mother's voice a mere whisper, reminding Nari she must not give in to anger when she wielded Serving magic. Anger did strange things to one's magic. She centered herself, choosing her spell carefully.

In one fluid motion, agile as a field cat, Nari withdrew her hand and gave Mordahn a hard shove. He yelped in surprise, toppling off the boulder. She shouted, "Bind Mordahn Erewin with magical cords; arms locked and feet shackled, for the next ten hours."

Mordahn's arms dropped to his sides as if glued in place. When he tried to get up, he stumbled to his knees. Tripping over his own feet, he found his ankles were bound with invisible cords, preventing him from doing more than shuffle a foot in either direction. He'd not be chasing after Nari again, leastwise, not for the next ten hours.

Mordahn sputtered angrily, "What game are you playing at?"

Nari folded her arms across her chest. "This is no game, Mordahn."

He struggled against the magical restraints, uttering oaths against her and her clan. Nari waited until he ran out of steam, until he slumped against the boulder, his mouth compressed in a tight line.

"Are you finished with your childish rant?" she asked. He glared at her and nodded. "Good, because now I want you to listen to me. I am neither a silly girl, nor your betrothed. I will never set foot on Arrowood land again, and you are unwelcome in Tanglewood, except to stand trial."

"Stand trial? What are you blathering about?"

Nari held up her hand, ticking off the reasons on her fingers. "First, you knew your father had turned away from Serving magic and yet you did not seek any assistance from my parents or the council, when we still might have been able to influence him. Second, you were aware of illegal crossbreeding within Arrowood and made no attempt to stop it or report it. Finally, you murdered an innocent woman in cold blood."

Mordahn drew his eyebrows down in an angry *V.* "Innocent? That fay creature killed my father."

"Her name was Elanya, and she did not kill your father. You shed innocent blood."

"But I was told...but I thought..." Mordahn dropped his head to his chest. When he looked up at Nari, she saw the same vacillation she'd seen earlier, remorse and regret warring with arrogance and pride.

Pawllah dashed out of the cave, her mass of braids

swishing behind her like a blue wave. She took in Mordahn slumped against a boulder, Nari standing over him with her arms crossed, and Pawllah nodded, a slow smile spreading across her face. "I see your magic's up to snuff again, lass. And not a moment too soon."

Nari heaved a sigh. "Too late, I'm afraid, for our dear friend." She pointed at the body lying under the copse of oak trees, and Pawllah gave an anguished cry. "Elanya! Oh Elanya!" Pawllah dashed over and dropped to her knees, weeping.

Nari noticed Mordahn kept his mouth shut, and she thought it was more out of fear at what Pawllah might do to him, than out of respect or even regret. Pawllah rose to her feet shakily, using a hand to steady herself against the nearest tree. Pawllah waved Nari over; she had something on her mind that she didn't want Mordahn to overhear.

Nari nodded, and then looked down at Mordahn, her finger pointed at his chest. "Stay." Of course, they both knew he had no choice. He'd not be breaking out of her spell, but somehow, Nari felt marginally better giving him that command.

He shot daggers at her with his eyes. "Don't fool yourself, Nari. You caught me off guard today, but you've won nothing. The battle lines are already drawn."

"What are you talking about? What battle lines?"

Mordahn tried to wave his hands but huffed at the invisible binds pinning his arms to his sides. "Our parents' deaths have stirred old hostilities. Arrowood and Riverwood don't trust the other clans, and Tanglewood, Shorewood, and Ridgewood don't trust us. The clans are itching for a war, and they'll have one. Unless..."

"Unless what?" Nari knew he was baiting her, but he'd piqued her curiosity. Besides, he might give away something useful.

Mordahn gave her a smile that showed too much teeth. "Unless the little Liege of Tanglewood and the new Chief of Arrowood perform the rites of binding."

"Are you trying to blackmail me into marriage to prevent a civil war?" she asked hotly, furious at herself for being drawn into conversation. Pawllah needed her. She had to wrap this up and be done with Mordahn.

"It's not blackmail," he said, shrugging, "merely political expediency."

"Never."

"So be it," he spat out. "The violence to come will be on your head then."

Nari fumed. "How dare you try to pin the blame for any infighting on me. It's your clan that's been dabbling in dark magic and crossbreeding and now, murder."

Mordahn's face hardened, his mouth a narrow slit. "Mark my words. You will never be our Liege. Arrowood and Riverwood are already rising up. Your uncle—"

"What about my uncle?"

Mordahn took a moment to examine his boots, drawing out the tension between them. Nari wanted to slap him, but she knew better than to go near him, despite his magical bindings. "I hear he's been assassinated inside your stronghold."

"You're lying." Nari blinked rapidly, tears prickling at her eyes. Of all her relatives, her mother's younger brother, Erick, was closest in age to her and by far the most fun-loving. She couldn't imagine anyone intentionally harming him. But then again, she'd have said the same thing a few days ago about her parents.

Mordahn shrugged. "You don't have to believe me. One of your fay friends will confirm it soon enough. But I can tell you this much: you will not have a moment's peace, anywhere in Faynwood. I'll make it my personal goal to hound you wherever you go." Nari felt a chill go through her, despite the warmth of the late spring evening.

Nari turned her back on him, unwilling to let Mordahn see how much he'd shaken her. Grabbing her sword from the ground, she hurried over to Pawllah, who had arranged Elanya's cape to cover her body. Nari was grateful. She'd seen enough death over the past few days. "I need to take Elanya home, but I don't want to leave you alone here with him." Pawllah took in Nari's trembling mouth and drew her brows together. "What's Mordahn been saying to you?"

Nari gave her a quick summary, Pawllah interrupting with a few grunts. Nari waited for Pawllah to refute Mordahn's claims, but her fay tutor shook her head. "We can only hope he's bluffing about your uncle."

"But what about the rest? Clan against clan?"

"Your mother's sleep had been disturbed of late, and not just with dreams of Orbahn's sorcery. She feared this, and your father too. The five clans have too many old grudges, old hostilities. One spark could ignite them, and what happened on the Arrowood road could have been that spark."

Nari thrust her hands into the pockets of her jacket. "If our stronghold has been compromised, then I can't go home, at least not anytime soon. And if Riverwood has thrown its support behind Arrowood, it's not safe to stay here."

Pawllah frowned. "After I return Elanya to our people, I'll transport us and our horses to Shorewood. Their chief will offer you protection until we figure something out."

Nari knew Pawllah meant well, but she also knew the fays had a different sense of timing. Pawllah might think she'd only be gone a few hours, but in fact, a few days could pass. Nari needed to take care of herself in the meantime. She wasn't about to babysit Mordahn, deep inside Riverwood territory, while she waited. She made up her mind. "Come find me after the funeral rites for Elanya. I'm heading to Valerra."

Faynwood shared a long, unguarded border with Valerra. Although Faymons rarely traveled beyond their own boundaries, Nari had heard stories about the strange, foreign land to the south. She knew about the cobblestone roads in Valerra's larger cities, where steam-powered vehicles known as locomobiles patrolled the streets. She'd heard the tales about strongholds without walls called estates, about buildings where live music and dramas were performed daily, and where farms and gardens were lush and green far longer than in Faynwood's harsher climate. She'd always thought it sounded magical, and as different from Faynwood as summer to winter.

"Valerra?" Pawllah narrowed her eyes thoughtfully, as if she were making up her mind about something. She finally nodded, warming to the idea. "They are strong proponents of Serving magic. But they're also distrustful of outsiders, especially Faymons with your blue-streaked hair and stronger magic. That could work in our favor, since they won't be forming alliances with rebel clans like Arrowood."

"How do Valerrans feel about fays?"

Pawllah waved her hand. "Many of them don't even believe we exist."

Nari's mouth dropped open. She couldn't imagine anyone not believing fays were real. Pawllah added, "Oh, they read all the old fay tales to their children, and they protect the fay artifacts in their possession. They have a strong sense of history. But a fay living in Valerra would have to use a glamour to hide her true nature."

"And your vivid blue hair." Nari crooked her finger at Pawllah's long blue braids.

"Aye, that too." Pawllah patted Nari's arm. "I need to go, but let's get you saddled up first. Another quarter hour isn't going to make a difference to poor Elanya."

Nari and Pawllah saddled both their horses and gently transferred Elanya to Pawllah's mare. Nari stepped away, giving a sad wave as the traveling mists encircled Pawllah, Elanya, and the horse, which neighed indignantly before being whisked away.

As Nari mounted Goldah, Mordahn called out. "Wait a minute. You're not going to leave me here, alone, without food or water?"

Nari pointed at the cave entrance. "I left you a bowl of water in the cave, which you'll be able to lap up, and a handful of nuts."

"How am I supposed to get there?" Mordahn pointed to his feet, with the invisible leg shackles.

She shrugged. "I guess you'll have to shuffle."

Mordahn snarled at her. "How dare you treat me like some dog? I'll never forgive you or your clan for this."

Nari squinted at her ex-fiancé. "Not like a dog, Mordahn. Like one of those grihms your father cross-bred." She picked up Goldah's reins and turned the sturdy palomino due south, away from Faynwood and Mordahn, away from warring clans and fresh betrayals.

Nari heard Mordahn ranting and swearing as she picked her way through the woods, his voice fading until all she could hear were the birds calling in the trees, and squirrels chattering in the branches. She searched for the trail Pawllah had told her about, which would keep her off the primary roads and lead her to Valerra.

Nari eventually found the marker described by Pawllah: an *L*-shaped maple, its trunk having been twisted by successive travelers when the tree was a young sapling. With a sigh of relief, she turned onto the thin ribbon of trail, little more than a bridle path. Nari loved the woods, even the unfamiliar trees of Riverwood, but she'd never traveled this far from home by herself. She wasn't afraid, not now that her magic was flowing again, but she felt so alone. Her parents dead, her homeland on the brink of civil war, even her fay tutor temporarily away.

Nari shook her head. She simply couldn't afford to dwell on her sadness. The weight of it threatened to crush her. Instead, she focused on searching for the trail markers; sometimes, the markers were another *L*-shaped tree, other times, a pile of stones that looked random, but in fact were cairns, hand-stacked by others passing through before her. That last thought gave her comfort. Although Valerra would be a very different place from Faynwood, and she would be an outsider, an immigrant with her blue-streaked hair and fay tutor, the more she turned the idea of Valerra over in her mind, the more it made sense.

Nari traveled until it was so dark she wouldn't be able to see the markers on the trail, and then she curled against the trunk of an enormous sequoia, Goldah resting nearby. She woke early, ate a handful of dried berries and nuts, and washed them down with some water from her water skin. Mounting Goldah, she continued following the trail, picking her way around fallen branches and pausing periodically to examine the cairns or crooked trees. By mid-afternoon, she noticed more sunlight filtering through the trees overhead.

Nari had reached the southern edge of Faynwood's densely wooded boundaries, where the towering sequoias, oaks, and maples started thinning out. She dismounted, guiding Goldah toward an outcropping of boulders. Beyond the boulders and the bluff on which she stood, gently rolling green hills, farms, and woodlands crisscrossed the countryside. "Valerra," she breathed. "It's beautiful, although it has nowhere near as many trees as Faynwood."

Nari patted Goldah's neck. "That's where we're going: Valerra. I don't know what we'll find, but I am sure of this—Mordahn and his father's Fallow magic won't be following us there."

"Let us hope you are right, my lady."

Nari jumped at the voice behind her, and then she spun around, a smile spreading across her face. "Pryl! You're recovered!" Closing the distance between them, Nari curled her arms around the fay in a friendly hug. While she expected Pryl to cough awkwardly, or clear his throat, or give her a stiff pat on the back, Pryl did none of these things.

Instead, he drew Nari into a fierce embrace, cradling her against his chest. "You're safe," he whispered into her hair. "Pawllah told me about Mordahn, and his threats. I came as soon as I could." Nari's heart sped up at Pryl's words and his strong arms encircling her. She inhaled his fresh, clean scent, a pleasing combination of sandalwood and petrichor.

Nari drew back and looked up at him. That's when she noticed Pryl's appearance. Rather than his sparkly silver cape and tunic, which marked him easily as a fay anywhere he traveled, Pryl was dressed like a wealthy foreigner, with dark blue trousers, an ivory linen shirt open at the collar, and a long brown leather cloak. He wore a navy trilby pulled low over his wavy hair, which wasn't vivid blue at all, but light brown. Nari tilted her head, her brow furrowed. "You're looking...remarkably well. But what happened to your hair?"

Pryl waved his hand. "Most Valerrans have absolutely no idea how to interact with fays. I'm dressed like one of them, and I cast a glamour to hide my hair color."

Something Pryl said surprised Nari, but in a good way. She'd had nothing but terrible surprises lately, so she was ready for a change. "You're coming to Valerra with me?"

Pryl nodded. Instead of staring at the ground, or at his boots, he looked directly into her eyes. "Of course. You'll be quite alone otherwise, other than Pawllah. Although she is brilliant and loves you dearly, I'm afraid she enjoys her wine a bit overmuch, and she is not very good with finances."

"She's not?"

Pryl shook his head. "Most definitely not. Don't tell her I said anything, but Pawllah's parents had to cover her debts several times over when she was younger. Although Pawllah's gotten better, you're still going to need help settling into your new life."

"And you're here to help me?" asked Nari, beginning to feel like a schoolgirl with all her questions. Then she recalled that moment sitting across the campfire from Pryl, before everything went so horribly wrong. The look they'd exchanged, the promise in his eyes. Maybe she hadn't imagined it at all.

Pryl reached over and brushed a lock of hair behind her ear. The gesture was both comforting and intimate. "Of course I'm here for you, as a friend..." Pryl hesitated and then took Nari's hands. "And more, when you are ready."

While this thing between them was totally unexpected, it was also something Nari knew she wanted to explore. She would take her time, without a doubt. But the more she thought about it, the more she liked the idea of Pryl in her life. Nari nodded. "I'm glad you'll be here with me." She looked down at her boots, feeling suddenly shy. "And as for the rest, let's take our time."

Pryl's shale gray eyes sparkled. "I will have no trouble waiting for you, my lady. When a fay knows what he wants, he can be very patient indeed." Pryl leaned over and gently brushed his lips against her cheek. Then taking her hand, he led Nari and their horses down the bridle path to Valerra.

PRYL

"I have a surprise for you." Pryl took Nari's hand and guided her out the door of the quaint hotel in Valerra's capital, where they'd been staying for the past few months. He'd paid for two bedroom suites, one for Nari, which she shared with Pawllah when the older fay visited, and a separate set of rooms for himself, one floor below Nari's to offer her maximum privacy.

After the ordeal she'd suffered—losing both her parents in a horrific assassination and then being pursued by her half-crazed ex-fiancé—Pryl knew she had to process her grief and fears at her own pace before true healing could take place. And he was determined to give Nari all the space she needed, for as long as she needed it.

Pryl would be as patient as he'd promised her on the rode to Valerra, but he yearned to enfold this brave, heartbroken woman in his arms and pledge his devotion. Unlike humans, who often broke their promises, when a fay gave himself to another, it was forevermore—a life-long oath.

He wanted to shower Nari with gifts, assure her she would be safe in Valerra, and show her she could trust another man again. He ached to kiss away every tear that trailed down her cheeks.

Instead, Pryl did the only thing he could: he waited for Nari to notice him, not as her ally or friend, but as her chosen mate. For he'd seen visions of them in the future, embracing each other, laughing often together, raising a family together, and hardest of all, weeping bitterly together. Pryl would take all the rawness and pain that life would throw their way, so long as he and Nari could share those sweet and tender moments as well.

And so he waited.

"Why do we need a buggy?" asked Nari, as Pryl helped her into the horse-drawn, open-air carriage that he'd rented for the day.

"I'm taking you for a picnic in the country," he replied, picking up the reins and guiding the pair of gray horses down the cobbled road. Of course, Pryl could simply have whisked Nari to wherever they wanted to go on his traveling mists, but not in the crowded city, where the human residents, even those with magic in their veins, had never encountered a fay before.

"What a thoughtful surprise. Did you conjure this perfect summer day as well?" Nari teased.

"The picnic is only a small part of your surprise.

You'll have to wait for the rest. And to answer your question, I haven't performed any spells yet today," said Pryl with a grin. Then he amended his statement. "Well, except for fixing my cravat, which is impossible to tie without magic. What a ridiculous human contrivance."

"I could show you how to tie your cravat." Nari smiled. "Without using any spells. Just say the word."

"Perhaps when I'm not driving a carriage," he answered wryly.

Nari chortled out loud. "Fair enough."

Pryl glanced over at Nari, laughing for the first time in weeks; it took all his fay-born willpower not to lean over and kiss her right then and there. Instead, he entangled the reins in his fingers, tapped his boots against the floor of the carriage, and fidgeted around in his seat, desperately hoping Nari liked his surprise, which signaled his commitment to her in a very big way, unlike anything he'd done to date.

Nari finally placed a hand on his arm. "What's got you squirming and jiggling like a nervous kitty?"

"Well..." Pryl sighed. "I did something truly out of character for me. You will probably think I'm impetuous after today, perhaps even a bit showy. But if you hate it, you must tell me."

"Well now you've gone and done it!"

"What do you mean?" Pryl asked, wondering whether he'd somehow managed to spoil the surprise before they even arrived.

"The anticipation is killing me," said Nari. "Can't you give me any hints?"

"I suppose I could give you one small hint," said Pryl. "I know how much you miss Tanglewood, with all its trees and gardens. We'll be picnicking in a rose garden today, although I warn you, it is quite overgrown."

Nari clapped her hands together. "Ooh, a rose garden? Is anything in bloom?"

"Aye, but there are also brambles, thorns, and weeds a plenty."

"Hmm, I wonder whether I could pull out some of those weeds whilst we're there? I yearn to work in a garden again." She peered down at her pale yellow day gown, which Pryl had purchased for her, along with the rest of her wardrobe. Nari Arlyss, who carried the blood of the Faymon Lieges in her veins, had literally fled her homeland with nothing but the clothes on her back. "Although I don't want to ruin my new gown."

"If you really want to do some gardening, I can make the arrangements and we can return another day. I happen to be on good terms with the owner. Would that please you?"

"Very much." Nari squeezed his arm. "You are too good to me."

Clasping the reins in one hand, Pryl reached over with his free hand and placed it briefly over hers. "I could never be 'too good' to you, my dear Nari." Then he took up the reins again and focused on the drive.

Before long they left the heart of the city behind them. The homes increased in size, more green parkland and wooded hills separating each estate, and Nari oohed at the various properties as they passed. Finally they came upon a bridle path that ran through a grove of trees growing so closely together they blocked the bright sunlight at times. Nari tried to get Pryl to tell her more about the rose garden where they'd be having their lunch, but he merely smiled and told her to be patient— which he'd learned was not one of Nari's strengths. She even pouted at one point, and he had to suck in his cheeks to keep his secret to himself a little bit longer.

They left the woods behind and turned up a gravel drive that wound past thick hedges of boxwood and yew trees so overgrown in places the driveway nearly disappeared. And then, finally, they rounded the last bend in the road and Nari gasped.

Sitting at the top of a low, green hill was a sad-looking, dilapidated mansion, its fluted columns dark with mold, half its windows and shutters missing, its wide staircase crumbling in several places.

Nari tilted her head at the house, her voice low, thoughtful. "It's a beautiful home, despite its state of disrepair. It must have been quite the sight, once upon a time. What's it called?"

"Delavan Manor," replied Pryl, pointing to an overgrown courtyard on the side of the mansion. "The rose garden is through there, although we'll need to pick our way carefully across the loose stones." He pulled up the horses, helped Nari down from the seat, and grabbed the picnic hamper from the back of the buggy.

Nari looped her arm through his, and a thrill ran through Pryl at the simple, trusting gesture. "I suppose the owner must be very old or possibly even deceased."

"Why do you say that?"

"Why else would anyone allow such an elegant home to fall apart like this?" Nari drew her brows together. "But wait a minute, didn't you say you knew the owner?"

Pryl cleared his throat. "Aye, that's true enough, although the place has only recently changed hands."

"Hmm…" Nari compressed her lips. "I'm not following."

Before Pryl could explain about the manor, and who the new owner was, and what was truly in his heart, a loud, deep "Woof!" pierced the air.

Nari turned toward the bark. "That sounds so much like—"

And then the largest mastiff in all of Faynwood broke through the unkempt yew trees, leapt over the scraggly boxwood, and sprinted toward Nari, who shrieked, "Quel! Is it really you?" She ran toward the beast, and dropping down to the grass, threw her arms around the yipping dog, who was so overjoyed he couldn't sit still long enough to be petted. Instead, he ran around in circles, whipping past Nari and Pryl like a fur-covered tornado.

Nari laughed, a deep, throaty laugh that made Pryl's heart swell with joy at the sound. She turned toward him, tears in her eyes. "You went to Tanglewood to retrieve him for me, didn't you?"

Pryl nodded, his throat too tight to speak.

"And my uncle Erick, is he…"

"He's fine," Pryl coughed, clearing his throat. "Erick

survived the assassination attempt, and he was over-joyed to know you were safe."

"Oh thank the stars! That's the best news we've had from home since...since all that's happened." Nari waved her hand to encompass the manor, woods, and gardens. "And what about this estate? *You* are the new owner, aren't you?"

This time Pryl shook his head, and Nari peered up at him, her brow creased in confusion. "But then—"

Pryl put the picnic hamper on the ground, gave Quel a warning look, and then took Nari's hands in his. "*You* are the new owner. I know it doesn't look like much right now, but—"

"Oh you dear, dear, man," Nari interrupted him, fresh tears moistening her eyes. "But why me?"

Pryl gingerly cupped Nari's face in his hands and peered into her eyes, waiting for her consent. When she nodded, he sealed his mouth over hers, shuddering at the sweetness of her lips mixed with the saltiness of her tears. He took his time, planting delicate kisses all along her jaw line and across her moist cheeks. When he finally broke away, he whispered, "I love you, Nari Ayala Arlyss. I fell for you the first time we met. You asked me whether I liked dogs, and I was so shy in your presence I choked on a scone."

Nari laughed. "I do remember wondering how you and Quel would get along. Come to think of it, you never did answer that question."

Pryl kissed the tip of her nose. "I adore dogs, cats,

griffins, dragons, and even gargoyles. Is there anything else you'd like to know?"

Nari nodded at the mansion behind them. "I hope you don't expect me to fix Delavan Manor all by myself?"

"Of course not," Pryl sputtered. "I thought we could work together on it, and since we're the only people for miles around, we could safely use magic to fix the most pressing issues. Once it's in better shape, I'll hire a staff to run it for you. I know it's not Tanglewood, but I think you could learn to like it here..." His voice trailed off when Nari arched an eyebrow at him.

"Let me rephrase my question," she said. "I hope you don't expect me to live in Delavan Manor all by myself, do you?"

"Ah, well, not precisely...I mean you will need a staff... and, um." Pryl stopped talking because now both Nari's brows were raised, and her dark eyes looked stormy. "Er, have I said something wrong?"

Nari shook her head at him. "You bought me a mansion with fay gold, retrieved my precious Quel from Tanglewood, told me you loved me, and kissed me until I nearly melted on the grass in a swoon, and yet you forgot something very important."

Pryl's brain had stopped working when Nari told him she'd nearly swooned from his kisses. *That's a good sign, isn't it? I must be doing something right.* Then he realized she said he'd forgotten something important. "What did I forget?"

"Isn't there a question you want to ask me?" Nari poked a finger in his chest.

His mind blanked out. *Unicorns and moonbeams! What have I forgotten?* He stared at Nari, furrowing his brow, a rising sense of panic squeezing his chest. "I...I..."

"I suppose this will be a sign of things to come." She sighed dramatically. "You'll go all silent and anxious at the most critical times, and I'll have to do the talking for both of us. Well, what do you have to say for yourself?"

"Er...well, um..." Pryl paused, unsure how to continue.

Nari rolled her eyes. "You're impossible A dear man, but truly impossible." She threw her arms around Pryl's neck and drew him down for a kiss that seared his lips, heated his insides, and left him panting for air. When she finally broke away, she placed her hands gently on either side of his face, and he closed his eyes, reveling in her touch.

But Nari was using his full fay name and asking him something very important, and so he forced his eyelids open. "Archipryllius Orion the Fourteenth, future Chief of the Fay Nation, will you complete the rites of binding with me?"

Pryl drew Nari into his arms, tipped up her chin, and whispered, "Just say when and where, and I am yours."

"Here and now," murmured Nari.

Pryl kissed her forehead. "Do you mind if we move our picnic to the fay realm? There's little chapel over-looking a valley of neon orange, lemon yellow, and shocking pink roses that I think you would enjoy as we recite our binding rites."

"Can Quel come?"

"Of course."

"Then what are we waiting for?" Nari's dark eyes twinkled with humor and a promise of so much more.

"Hang tight, my love," said Pryl, wrapping an arm around her waist and whistling for the giant mastiff, who bounded over to join them.

A swirl of vaporous tendrils encircled Nari, who gripped Quel's collar, and Pryl, who scooped up their picnic hamper. Then they vanished in a puff of mist, Quel's deep bark and Nari's accompanying laughter echoing across the wide, green lawn.

BOOKS BY TONI CABELL

A fast-paced adventure full of magic, romance, humor, sword fighting, dangerous creatures, and the power of light versus darkness, **Serving Magic** is a YA Epic Fantasy series with Steampunk and Regency vibes. Winner of The Wishing Shelf Book Awards and recognized by Indies Today as a Top 5 YA Fantasy series by an indie author:

- *Lady Apprentice, Book 1*
- *Lady Mage, Book 2*
- *Lady Liege, Book 3*
- *Lady Spy, Book 4*
- *Lady Reaper, Book 5*

In the arid hills of Toresz, there's one thing more dangerous than divining for water... falling in love with the enemy. **Water Witch** is YA Romantasy duology packed with action, danger, intrigue, royal politics, and romance. Winner of The Wishing Shelf Book Awards:

- *The Lightness of Water, Book 1*
- *The Way of Water, Book 2*

If you're looking for sweet, slow-burn romance with swoony kisses, second chances, and funny, heartwarming characters, don't miss the complete **Faeries of Door County** series. Winner of Best Paranormal Romance, each novel is a standalone story set in the same cozy small town:

- *Rhyme, Riddle, and Romance*
- *Half a Faerie*
- *Return to Mooncrest Inn*

Find all Toni's available books and upcoming new releases on tonicabell.com and Amazon. All her novels are also available in audiobook format on Audible and Apple Books.

About the Author

When Toni told her fifth-grade teacher that she wanted to be a writer, neither of them expected Toni's journey to include stints as a nurse's aid, personal banker, instructional designer, real estate broker, systems analyst, and youth director. Toni is thrilled to be an indie author and does at least half her writing in the middle of the night, which may explain her wild plot twists and unforgettable characters.

Today, Toni writes award-winning fantasy stories filled with spunky gals, protective guys, imaginative magic, and romance that sizzles without the spice. Whether you're a fan of fast-paced, YA fantasy adventures with a dash of swoon or cozy paranormal romance packed with heart-stealing kisses and small town charm, you're sure to find something to love.

Toni's novels have earned Silver and Bronze Medals in The Wishing Shelf Book Awards, two Gold Medals in the Global Book Awards, and Best Paranormal Romance from Indies Today.

She makes her home in a small village along the shores of

Lake Michigan with her handsome husband, where she enjoys generous supplies of strong coffee, too many pastries, and more books than she can ever read.

Want a free novella and to stay current on Toni's upcoming releases, sales, and giveaways? Then visit toni cabell.com and sign up for her newsletter.

Toni posts regularly about her indie author journey, life lessons, what inspires her, and her books on Instagram and Facebook. Also consider joining her Reader Group on Facebook, @onceuponaswoon, where she hangs out with some of her closed-door author friends and readers like you.

Soli Deo Gloria.